I0623035

WEB OF THE ATRAX

KENNETH PASSAN

SEVERED PRESS
HOBART TASMANIA

WEB OF THE ATRAX

ISBN: 978-1-925711-45-5

This book is dedicated to my wife, Gayle, who hates spiders as much as I do.

Scientific Classification

Kingdom: Animalia
Phylum: Arthropoda
Subphylum: Chelicerata
Class: Arachnida
Order: Araneae
Infraorder: Mygalomorphae
Family: Hexathelidae
Genus: Atrax
Species: A. robustus

The itsy bitsy spider climbed up the waterspout
Down came the rain and washed the spider out
Out came the sun and dried up all the rain
So the itsy bitsy spider climbed up the spout again

From children's nursery rhymes

PROLOGUE

December 4-Summer, Maitland, New South Wales, Australia

It was a hot, blistering day in the field right outside of his home. Forty-eight year old Ken Walker was no stranger to these 90 plus temperatures, however. His tanned weathered face bore the direct results from working so much outdoors. But he was an outdoor kind of guy anyway. He never could stand sitting around inside doing basically nothing because he didn't believe in that. Besides, he had a farm to run, albeit a small one. Small or large, however, it was a responsibility he took seriously and knew he couldn't afford not to work hard to keep it going.

Even though it was still officially spring until the 21st, as far as he was concerned it was summer. He was readying for the harvest of his corn. Already 80 degrees at 7:00 am, he was ready to harvest some of his corn that he'd planted only 6 months before. Seemed like it was just yesterday.

As a bachelor, he never really had time to womanize. He liked women but he was more dedicated to his work than establishing a permanent relationship. He had friends, including women. A couple of them had put feelers out to see if he would take the hint, but he never took anyone's hint. That's the way he was. He didn't reject anyone because he socialized well-enough. But he preferred not to have the distractions of a relationship, at least not right now.

Living alone on a moderate sized farm could be a lonely life for most people. At times, he did feel a need for some companionship. Those times would be mostly at night when the work was done for the day and he used the evenings for resting and relaxing. It gave him a lot more time to think about what he was easily able to avoid thinking about during the day when his work took up all his concentration and focus.

His six foot two inch tall lanky frame was certainly not frail. In fact, he was pretty strong with muscles that didn't stand out like a body builder's, yet bore the strength of one. He could be attractive to any female with interested eyes. He certainly wouldn't mind that at all. But keeping his farm going meant everything to him. It was his life, his work, and his livelihood. Without it, where would he go? Besides, it was passed down in the family from generation to generation and he was not going to be the first one to break from the family's farm life. He enjoyed it. Maybe someday the right woman would come along and would want to be a part of it and of him. In the future, well, who knows? Maybe when he felt he was ready he would consider it.

For now, he walked through a small portion of his cornfield to check on some of his plantings. Most of them looked ripe and ready for the picking, at least on the outside. He picked one off the stalk and removed the covering. It was a yellow-white coloring with no blemishes. He took a bite, chewed it a bit and then spit out the mouthful. Smiling, he felt satisfied. This was good corn and he was pleased with himself.

Unfortunately, not all the corn came out like that. A few seemed to be resistant to growth and development. Every so often he'd come across one that should have been fully developed but somehow the process got caught up in some genetic cogwheel that either slowed down or stopped the process. As a result, the ear would be no good to eat, although he could feed it to the couple of pigs he had. Those were the only animals he would keep on the farm. His main focus was on corn and other vegetable crops.

He decided it was unnecessary to check out any more like that. After walking through a little more of the field, he turned and retreated in the direction he came from. It was time to get the corn harvester.

The barn he kept it stowed in was just fifty yards away. Leisurely strolling over to it, he wiped the sweat off his brow. Even at this early morning hour, the air temperature indicated a hot day. Not unbearable, but not a day to do real strenuous activity outside either. But he didn't regard running the corn harvester as strenuous activity. In fact, he enjoyed it, although he knew he'd have to take a break now and then to hydrate and shade himself inside for a few minutes before he continued. He was alone so no one was pushing him to continue or to stop. Still, he was wise enough to know to be careful outside when it was this hot. The Australian sun could be unforgiving if you let it.

The barn was the usual, stereotypical type with lots of room on the ground level where one might keep hay or equipment. In this case it was the latter. There was a loft also and a ladder leading up to it. He kept smaller equipment and other miscellaneous items up there that he didn't use on a regular basis. Every now and then he'd go up there and grab something.

Because of the size of his farm, it was quite a bit of work for one person. It was left to him by his parents who passed several years ago. His mother had died about ten years ago from pancreatic cancer at the age of 64. Five years later his father had died from cirrhosis. Unfortunately, his drinking had shortened his life considerably. Ken realized what happened to his father and decided that he would not allow that to happen to him. He knew that alcoholism could run in the family and so, bound and determined, he never started drinking. He valued his life too much.

So here is all his pride and joy, and he's making it work, having sold a satisfactory amount of corn last year. Now with the corn harvester in front of him, he was readying it for operation. After checking the oil level and making sure it was fueled up, he was prepared to start the engine when he spotted something on the floor across the way. It was softball sized and black. He hadn't seen that before. Curiosity made him stroll over to it. He immediately saw what it was: a black bird, dead on the floor.

What the hell, he thought. He looked up to see if it had flown through a hole in the roof. He didn't see one which confirmed the fact that the open barn door had been the way it got in. That was ok as far as he was concerned. There was nothing in here he could imagine it would want. Why it was dead here was a mystery. It could have easily flown back out, so entrapment was certainly not an issue.

After briefly examining it, he looked around for a rag or something. He didn't have anything to pick it up with so he'd have to do it manually. But he didn't want to use his bare hands. After going to the work bench at the closed end of the barn, he picked up and donned his work gloves. Returning back to the bird, he bent down to pick it up off the floor, failing to notice a web-like structure, close to the dead bird that peeked out from a small depression on the dirt floor under an old board.

As he grabbed the bird, something lightning quick appeared, something softball sized and black like the bird, except with lots of legs. He felt sudden excruciating pain in his right hand and yelled out like never before. He quickly removed the thick glove and could see what looked like puncture marks on the top of his hand between his thumb and forefinger. There appeared a drop of blood near the marks. Something had bitten him right through the glove.

"Aww!!! Awww, son of a bitch!" he screamed to no one but himself. No one could hear him because his nearest neighbor was a mile away. He shook his hand vigorously, hoping the pain would subside within the next couple of minutes. But it didn't. What he actually had just done was made it worse.

Not imagining what it could possibly have been that either bit or stung him, he looked down to see if he could find what it was. And that's when he saw it just outside some kind of web structure. It was terrifying in appearance and looked like it was standing on its hind legs with its forelegs raised high in the air. He could see what looked like huge fangs hanging straight down, slightly curved inward.

He knew it was a spider, but had no idea what kind. Australia had lots of creepy crawlies, including a smorgasbord of spiders. A number of them were pretty scary looking, but most were not harmful or deadly to humans. He figured this was probably one of them and he just happened to run into it by chance. Without much further thought, he ran forward and immediately squashed it with his shoe. "There, you conniving bug, that's what you deserve," he yelled at it. Then a wave of pain even worse than before hit him and it almost floored him right there.

Deciding to go to the house immediately, he thought he better wash it with cold water, figuring that might help the pain. When he tried that under the kitchen faucet, he discovered it didn't work. He went to sit down, grabbing a cold soda from the fridge and then holding his hand.

He waited a few minutes, believing the pain would subside after a little time had passed. He didn't have a clue as to what was happening inside of him. In the past he'd been stung by bees and wasps and creepers. He'd even been stung by a spider, although a considerably smaller one than the one that just got him. That actually didn't mean too much considering that even some small spiders can pack a painful punch. Nevertheless, he got over all of those stings surviving with flying colors. Why should this be any different just because the thing was bigger? he thought. So he sat and waited.

The pain didn't go away. In fact, it continued to get worse. He started noticing goose bumps on his arms, although he was, for now, oblivious to the increased sweating he was having. The house was air conditioned. A few minutes later, he felt tingling around the mouth and tongue and started salivating. That's when the alarm bell rang in his head. This was not normal and he became immediately concerned. Going to the phone, he called for an ambulance and explained his situation to the emergency operator, after which he gave his name and address.

"Sir, do you know what kind of spider it was?"

"No, ma'am I don't. All I know it was big and black."

Punching this into her computer, the emergency dispatch operator pressed him for more information.

"About how big was it?"

He told her.

"Describe it as completely and as accurately as you can."

Between the waves of pain and mouth twitching, he was able to give her as best a description as he could. She punched it into her computer as he talked. He found that talking was becoming more difficult and he told her so.

After a few more seconds, she gave him some instructions.

"Sir, I'm going to ask you to either lie down or sit down and move as little as you can. I've called for Lifeflight to come get you. You will need to get to hospital as quickly as possible. Please remain as calm as you can. The helicopter is readying for takeoff now, even as we speak. Are you experiencing any further symptoms in addition to what you described?"

He told her he was feeling increased anxiety and what seemed like heart palpitations, although he wasn't totally sure because he had never experienced them before. "I don't like this tingling and numbness, ma'am. That really bothers me. Do you know what could have stung me?"

The operator had a good idea what it was, but she didn't want to say on the phone. The man was distressed enough without causing him more emotionally.

"I'm not sure, Mr. Walker because I'm not a spider expert. But be assured that you're getting the help in plenty of time. Someone at the hospital might be able to tell you. The main thing is for us to focus on getting rid of your symptoms and underlying problem. That will be done there. Just be sure to move around as little as possible."

"Ok, operator." Ken started huffing a little, with a slight increase in breathing difficulty. "How long 'til the chopper gets here?"

"About 10 to 15 minutes the most. Can you hang on 'til they get there?"

Ken grimaced, feeling the onset of tightness in his chest. As the invasion through his veins took hold, current symptoms were worsening. "I guess..." He took some heavy breaths, "... I guess I'll have to, won't I?"

"Just stay on the line, Ken. I'll stay here with you until they get there. When they do, let me know and I'll hang up. Ok?"

Even as she spoke, the operator was fearful for the man on the other end. This was not good. He was becoming less communicative on the phone and soon he wasn't talking at all or responding to any of her questions or remarks.

"Sir? Sir? Mr. Walker, Ken, can you hear me? Are you still there?"

The operator could only hear some soft humming in the distance. Other than that, the phone was silent. Then she heard his voice, which was considerably weaker than before. She thought she heard him say "help me" which sounded more distant and slurred.

"Oh dear God," the operator muttered softly. She contacted the Lifeflight crew and told them that the subject was now unresponsive and to take great care on entering the house where he was located. She knew he had been bitten by something probably deadly- a spider or, she was thinking- possibly the eastern brown snake which was reputed to be one of the most toxic venomous snakes in the world. He hadn't said where that happened. For all she knew, it could have been in the house. The pilot rogered her and said their ETA was now five minutes. It would be a long five minutes. Unfortunately for Ken Walker, it would be an eternity.

1

December 5, Canberra, New South Wales

"Sandy, let's go. Hurry up. Your school bus is almost here."

For Tabitha Ingram, it was another typical school and workday morning. Fortunately this was one of her days off from her waitress job, so she could concentrate more on getting Sandy off before the bus came and left her. She really didn't feel like driving Sandy to school just because she wasn't ready on time.

Sandy was trying to rush, running around in her room, gathering up whatever she could to take to school with her. If she could have, she would have taken all the toys in her bedroom.

"Ok, mommy, I'm ready."

The little girl was as she said she was. Her long blond hair was pulled back into a ponytail and she wore her little white dress with the small pink bow on the front. It looked cute on her.

"Ok, let's get out there. Here's your lunch box."

Sandy took it and with her mom, walked out to the bus stop at the curb in front of their house. Together they watched it approach them. She liked to take the bus, thinking it was fun. She got to look at all the houses and everything going by and talk to some of her school friends at the same time. Soon, she got on the bus waving goodbye to her mom and was off to school for the day. It was another sunny day in Canberra. Tabitha returned to the house. Her husband, Peter, had already gone off to work, having to be at the plant by 7:00 am. His job as a mechanical engineer over in Rellington, just a few miles from their home, kept his family well in the black financially. Although Tabitha didn't have to work at all, she chose to waitress part time just for the enjoyment of helping people and have a tad of socializing at the same time. On her days off, she would make sure the house was kept clean and neat.

The Ingrams lived in a moderately upscale neighborhood of the capital city, more on the outskirts than in the city itself. There the houses were moderate to large-sized with mowed and well-kept lawns but without picket fences. The neighbors all watched out for each other and the neighborhood watch kept safety at a priority level. There was very little to no crime here, which made everyone feel safe and happy.

The day was warm and getting warmer, with the sun making the weather pleasant and hot at the same time. As with most other places in

New South Wales, they had their fair share of rainy days as well as sunny days.

Inside, Tabitha used some of the morning time to straighten out and put some items away that had been out for a while but not used. She did everything possible to avoid clutter. By keeping up with this and other things on her days off, she was able to maintain the neatness of the house much easier and with less work to do.

The Ingram house was a two story typical raised ranch style home. Being on the large end of house sizes, it had three full bedrooms, two bathrooms, a well sized kitchen with a round built-in bar table in the center and a significant amount of counter space. The modern digital stove and oven had the built-in microwave over it. In essence, she had more than enough room for preparing full meals for the family.

Sandra, or Sandy as she preferred to be called, was their only child, now 11 years old. Unfortunately, before they could provide her with a little brother or sister, Tabitha had developed a cyst on one of her ovaries and then later the other one. With complications accompanying the normally benign problem, both of them had to be removed. As a result, she could have no more children, unless they adopted. It was initially devastating, more for her than for Peter, but she eventually accepted that. In the end, they were grateful to at least have Sandy.

Going from one room to another, she picked up a few loose items around and what was on the floor. Gathering the laundry in the bedrooms, she brought the baskets to the laundry room on the basement level and put them in the washer. Before she started back up the stairs the phone rang. She picked up the laundry room extension.

"Hello?"

"Yes hi Tabitha. This is Katherine, Katherine Beasley from Hurley's." Hurley's was the restaurant she worked at. Katherine was the manager there.

"Oh hi, Kathy. How are ya? What's up?"

"We have a bit of a problem. Two people called out sick today. I know it's your day off and I am really sorry to bother you, luv. Have to ask anyway. Wondering if you have the time to come in for three to four hours today to help out? That is, if you don't already have plans. If you do, that's ok. I can still call others. If you don't, we can sure use your help."

Tabitha thought for a minute. "Well, I'm doing laundry right now. Can't leave until it's done. What time are you talking about?"

"How about one to four this afternoon? I promise I won't keep you after four."

Tabitha quickly searched the calendar in her mind for any possible appointments today. She remembered there were none. As with the days she was scheduled to work, she would have the Johnsons next door watch Sandy until she returned home from the restaurant. She told Kathy she'd have to check with them first because today was her day off. She couldn't just assume they'd be able to watch her.

After advising Kathy she'd call her back with her answer, she called the Johnsons and was told that wouldn't be a problem. They would meet Sandy at the bus when it came. After thanking Sue Johnson, she called Kathy back and the arrangement for her to work was made.

While the washing machine was going, she tidied up herself for the day, and applied her makeup. She didn't need to dress for the job until later. It only took about fifteen minutes for her to get to work. After finishing up in the bathroom, she settled down to relax in the kitchen with a cup of coffee. Although she preferred tea, some mornings she craved coffee instead. That would satisfy her craving until the next time, which could be in two or three days.

In the laundry room, the machine was agitating, getting close to the first rinse cycle. It was now 7:50 am. Sandy had been gone for ten minutes, Peter about an hour and a half.

The laundry room had an exit door which had stairs leading to the outside, as a basement would. Technically it was part of the basement, but she kept it looking more like a separate room than a cellar. It was tile floored with wood-paneled walls.

She had been unaware that the door was about two to three inches ajar. She hadn't noticed it when she was down there. If she had, she might not have been too concerned anyway. There were too many more important things she needed to focus on rather than an open door. Besides, the outer door at the top of the stairs she knew to be definitely locked. Security was not a concern for her.

Being half underground, the laundry room/cellar was always cooler than the rest of the house. When it was first built about ten years ago, it began as a crawl space which could only be used for limited storage. Later Peter decided they really needed a full basement and so hired contractors to build one. Because there wasn't a lot of room upstairs for a washer and dryer, he decided it might be a good idea to make part of it a laundry area, which would be ideal. Only carrying the baskets of clothes and linen would be an issue but such a minor one that it was soon brushed aside as being no issue at all.

She didn't like just sitting and watching the machine working. As it was doing its job, she would go upstairs to keep busy with other things which were minor necessities, such as wiping the table or the counters and making sure the sink was clear of all dirty dishes and cups. They had a dishwasher which she used occasionally, although she didn't always use it. When she did, it was because she was too tired to wash dishes manually or sometimes she just didn't feel like washing by hand.

After about another twenty-five minutes, she figured the washer was done. Time to throw them into the dryer. After drying her hands, she plopped the towel down and headed back downstairs.

Going directly to the washer and dryer, she missed the small movement in the three inch wide open doorway which revealed only darkness.

The spinning in the washer was slowing down now. Opening the lid, she took the wet spun clothes out and threw them through the open door of the dryer. After making sure all the clothes were out, she closed the washer lid, and started the dryer going. Another set of clothes done, she thought to herself. *Well done, Tabby.* Actually, this being a typical day meant it was the standard mundane day of a stay at home housewife. She didn't mind it though because it gave her plenty of time to keep the house clean with no rushing around. Only her call to work a few off-hours made this day different than her other off days. Besides, that three hours would go by fast.

2

December 6, Newcastle, New South Wales

It was a Saturday morning. John Hampton was already outside mowing the lawn and would afterward, as he had planned, do some trimming around the grass perimeter. The day was typical, with partly cloudy skies. There was a threat of rain later on in the day which was one reason he was out at 8:00 am to start the yard work.

He was a retired carpenter, having worked most of his young life with wood and building things because he had enjoyed it. It was such a passion for him that even outside of work, he would build things from small stockpiles of wood he kept in his shed. His wife, Norma, was not so outdoorsy, so she maintained the inside of the house and took care of all the usual necessities of suburban living. Although he was in his late 60s, he maintained his good health and was quite physically fit for his age. Sometimes he tended to overdo it on the work and overexerted himself. When Norma noticed this, she would always remind him of his limitations and to watch himself because he was no spring chicken anymore.

After he finished mowing the lawn, John took his weed whacker out of the garage and started trimming the perimeters around the lawn, bushes, and the two trees they had in their front yard. When he stopped the machine briefly, he heard a voice calling out to him.

"John. Dear, would you like a glass of juice or lemonade?"

John wiped the sweat off his face. It was already getting pretty warm outside, although not more than the typical day's heat. He was feeling thirsty, now that Norma mentioned lemonade.

"Yea, I think so. I'll take a glass of lemonade, hon."

He scanned the nearby areas where he would continue the trimming and decided to work at the bushes right in front of the house while Norma went to get his drink. Starting up the machine, he started trimming down the weed undergrowth from one of the bushes, when he spotted something large and black. He couldn't tell for sure what it was because it was mostly hidden under a few dead leaves.

Bending down to take a closer look, he realized that it was alive, whatever it was because he saw it move back a little on its own. Not knowing what it was for sure, he was not foolish enough to try and grab the thing with his bare hands. Instead, he took the stem of the weed whacker in his hands. Without starting it up, he poked and prodded gently at the leaves covering the thing.

"Here ya go, luv. Nice and cold," she said outside her front door. "What ya doing there?"

She had seen him poking at something with the machine off and was curious.

With whacker in hand, he briefly left the front bush area to get his drink and took a gulp of it. "Hmm, that's good. Just what I needed."

"Find something in the bushes, did ya?" she asked.

"Don't know. Saw something there. I need to check it out. Let me finish this so I can go find out what it is. I don't want to leave this outside for the bugs." Finishing it up, he returned back to the bushes where he saw the thing.

When he looked, it appeared to be gone.

"Damn, what the hell was that?" he said out loud softly. He didn't like things left undone and oftentimes his curiosity took over the rest of any rationale he exhibited. He started poking around again. Then he stopped and realized that he had something better for this job than the weed whacker. Putting it down, he went and fetched the small wooden iron-toothed rake from the tool shed and started immediately prodding around that dirt area near the large bush.

He saw the exact spot where that thing had been but it was gone. He prodded the leaves apart but it wasn't there anymore. Looking up further, he scanned underneath the front door steps. It wasn't a solid cement structure of steps but was made of solid wood which left a space underneath it. He looked under that space but, of course, didn't see anything. Being the stubborn and persistent type of person, he decided to look underneath the steps to see if it had gone there.

Prodding with the rake, he poked and prodded at more dead leaves and twigs within the shadows there. He thought he saw movement from further back. Then he spotted something quite odd that he had never seen before. It looked like some kind of very thin, white netting. It wasn't real obvious and could have been very easily missed if he hadn't been concentrating on that area. He saw it twitch slightly and very briefly, barely noticeable.

"My my," he said softly under his breath. "What have we here? Seems to be my day for finding things."

He prodded gently at the white netting or web, whatever it was. As he poked further, he discovered that it seemed to have a hollow inside to it.

Weird, he thought.

He poked in further with the end of the handle while holding the metal rake in his hand. As more leaves moved and shifted positions, he discovered that the white netting was considerably larger than he thought. It actually seemed to extend about a foot or foot and a half further back and looked like it narrowed toward the other side, something like a funnel. He didn't see if anything was inside, but then suspected that something like this had to be built by something. He just didn't know what. Then it hit him.

Pulling the end of the handle back toward its exit, he realized that this was likely some kind of web, spider web most likely. It was a huge web so he suspected its resident to be other than small. He wasn't a bug enthusiast and hated most creepy crawlies, so he started to back off. As he did, something large and black ran out of the web entrance with lightning quickness and before he could lift the handle up, started running up the handle to him. He saw the two to three-inch largeness of it and screamed as he immediately threw the rake out of his hands and ran to the end of his yard.

"Holy Moly! Oh my God, what the hell was that?" he yelled out loud.

Norma came running out the door. "John, what's the matter? What happened?" She saw his white face and knew something had scared him. But what?

"Whew. That was one nasty looking thing. Huge spider, I'd say. I know we have a bit of nasty critters around these parts but, man, that thing was really nasty looking. Makes me wonder if I should go out and buy a six inch cannon."

"Oh, Dear, don't be ridiculous. Might want to get a pic of it next time you see so maybe we can show that to someone who knows what it is."

"Pic you say?" John shook his head. "No, I don't think so. I'll be lucky if the thing doesn't chase me down. That thing moved fast. And there's one thing I do my best to stay away from, and that's creepy critters that move fast. C'mon I'm going back inside for a minute to get something to drink. Already it's hotter than blazes out here."

As he started going back in the house, he looked back at the rake and the handle, wondering what would have happened if the thing had gotten to him. Without a second thought, he was back inside where it was nice and cool.

3

December 4, Sydney Memorial Hospital

By the time the chopper had delivered Ken Walker to the emergency department, his vital signs were dangerously low and significantly life-threatening. When they checked all his other signs, nurses and trauma doctors found his pupils to be fixed and dilated. Although he was unconscious, there was generalized muscle twitching, especially in his extremities. His right hand and fingers were extremely swollen and looking blown up like a balloon. Some of the swelling had invaded his wrist area and it was very red as well.

One of the doctors asked loudly to no one in particular. "Does anyone know what bit him?"

No one knew for sure. However, one of the other doctors seemed to have a gut feeling of what it was because he had seen something like this a few years before. It was not something he believed he would ever forget.

"Yea. It could have been the Funnel Web. Maybe the Sydney type, I'm not sure."

The doctor who asked looked at him in with obvious concern. "Funnel Web?" he asked, in a tone that required a confirming reply. "Are you sure? Tell me you're just kidding or that you could be wrong."

"No, I'm not kidding. I can't be sure, but I have seen someone else like this a few years back. He just about died several times, but survived in the end because of the antivenin in addition to very close medical monitoring. They happened to have it on hand."

The doctor in charge, Dr. Ian Williamson, ordered immediate IV normal saline hydration and had someone call for the antivenin. "I want ten bottles of the stuff, stat, " he told the caller. As the caller picked up the phone to call the appropriate office there, he added, "And tell them we need it yesterday. This man's life depends on it."

The hospital kept a supply of various antivenins in a particular locked area of the hospital. These substances, although toxic, could save lives. The catch was to find the right one for the right envenomation. Even if the right antivenin was found, there was no guarantee it would work. In fact, it could even kill the patient. In most cases, it was the patient's only chance. He or she would die without it.

The caller was soon talking to someone on the other end. As she spoke with the antivenin technician, medical personnel did all they could for the patient. He was quickly hooked up to monitors that automatically recorded his heart rate, respiration, blood pressure, and blood saturation level. He would remain on the monitor until this problem was resolved.

The doctors knew that the odds were now stacked against the patient. Williamson asked one of the nurses to call for a spider specialist and get him on the phone pronto. He was no expert on this kind of arachnid, or any arachnid for that matter. It was imperative that he know what he was up against right now.

It was so rare now for a patient to die of a spider bite because of the availability of appropriate antivenins that this case caught everyone off guard there. Presently, he didn't know if the patient's condition was exhibiting symptoms of early stage envenomation or the end stage. After looking up the number, the nurse called the University of Australia at Canberra to try and get a spider specialist on the line. Did such a person fall under the category of Entomology? She suspected so. She knew that university had such a department.

#

December 5, Canberra, New South Wales
It was nearly 9:30 am and Tabitha had almost forgotten about the clothes. She had been busy trying to sew a button back on to a blouse she needed to wear for work. After she finally got it back on the blouse, she arranged the blouse neatly on the bed and went for another cup of coffee. For some reason she had more than a normal urge for coffee today. Making up her mind this would be her last cup of the day, she went to the kitchen to fix it up, took a swig, put it down on the table and went downstairs to see if the clothes in the dryer were done yet.

Turning the small TV on which they kept down there, she listened to the news as she removed the clothes from the dryer. As she sorted, her attention was brought to what was being said on the TV.

"This just in. Forty-eight-year-old Kenneth Walker, a farmer from the outskirts of Maitland who was allegedly bitten by the Sydney Funnel Web spider yesterday while working in his barn died today at Sydney Memorial Hospital. When emergency transport personnel had arrived by helicopter at his home, he was already unconscious. Roger Flemming has the rest of the story." The screen then flipped to the reporter at Walker's home.

"Tom, this could only be described as a sad tragedy that could have happened to anyone. Although it wasn't initially known where he was bitten when Mr. Walker arrived at the hospital because he was unconscious, he had woken up briefly and was able to describe what happened and where it happened. As medical personnel waited for the antivenin to arrive, Ken Walker submerged into unconsciousness once again, this time not waking up. By the time the antivenin arrived, it was too late. Despite concerted efforts to revive him, they were not able to. An autopsy will reveal exactly what happened to him medically."

"There in the barn," the reporter said while pointing to the structure, "is where he says he was bitten. Bites from these spiders are often fatal. However, with appropriate and prompt treatment, most victims can survive. Unfortunately for Ken Walker, they suspect he had waited too long to call for help and in the end it was too late to save him. Roger Flemming, 7News, back to you Tom."

Tabitha stopped working with the clothes and became mesmerized with what she was seeing and hearing on the news. She'd never heard of this happening before, at least not in this general area. She walked over to it to listen to more of what the news was about to say.

Tom Banson, the anchorman was now speaking again. "To find out a little more about this particular spider, 7News has Dr. Angela Mayberry with us, a noted entomologist with the Australian Department of Parks and Wildlife." The camera then spotlighted the young dark-haired specialist to its viewers, then showed both of them.

"Dr. Mayberry, can you tell us a little about this particular spider? Why would it have killed this latest victim and no one else, at least that we know of?" The camera now focused on her.

"First of all, we know that Mr. Walker didn't get treatment in time to save him. A large part of the reason for that is likely due to delay in calling for help.

"This was almost certainly the species of spider Atrax robustus, otherwise known as the Sydney Funnel Web spider. It is one of the most toxic and dangerous species on the planet. Although there are other subspecies of the funnel web, this is considered one of the most dangerous.

"Its symptoms come on fast and furious which, among many other things, often involve seizures. It's very aggressive and positions itself in a terrifying attack position when it feels threatened. It will not hesitate to attack anything, including humans. Its venom is a powerful neurotoxin that can cause all kinds of breathing and muscular problems as well. Without proper and prompt treatment and antivenin, it can be fatal. Fortunately, antivenin is usually readily available or quickly available under most circumstances. That means most people can survive this."

"Doctor, what can a person do to avoid these creatures in the first place?" asked Tom.

Tabitha went back to sort more clothes out and then fold some of them. She had taken the two items that couldn't go in the dryer initially and hung them on a wooden clothes rack to air dry. The low humidity down there would help them dry better.

"...cool, dry places. Make sure all doors are closed to the outside to prevent them from entering homes. Spaces under doors leading to the outside should be..."

Without really listening anymore, she shut the TV off now that the latest bit of news was broadcast, noticed the door ajar and closed it. She felt bad about the man dying and didn't want to think too much about why that happened. She hated bugs and didn't want to also think about them, so she tuned them out. Something like that wasn't going to happen to her or her family. She didn't live on a farm out in the boonies. Without further thought about it, she brought the dry clothes back upstairs. She didn't think that she had forgotten to turn the TV off down there until she was halfway up the stairs. But with the basket of clothes in her hand, she sighed and decided to come back down after she put those away. The TV could wait for five minutes.

4

December 5, Newcastle, New South Wales

"I tell ya one thing, darlin'. I'm not taking anythin' for granted anymore. Heavy gloves from now on out there. Sometimes with those things, where there's one, there's lots more."

Norma put her hand on her chest. "My Lord, the way you screamed I thought you were being attacked by a bull elephant."

"Whew," he exclaimed. "Never seen anything like *that* before."

"I know sweetheart. You said that already. Better enjoy your break and get your bearings before something else jumps out at you." After he downed the glass of lemonade, John decided to put the matter aside and get back outside. He still had work to do.

Getting the lawnmower from the shed, he checked the fuel tank and saw it needed some petrol. Grabbing the can, he started filling it. He usually refilled it before each job because he didn't like to do it when the machine was still hot from running. He thought he heard footsteps from behind him and turned his face to look over his shoulder.

"Hey there, mate. Everything all right here?" the man said, gently slapping John on the shoulder. He turned around and saw his neighbor, Sam Winfield. "Heard you yelling. Had to make sure you're alright. You didn't get bitten by anything did ya?"

John looked at Norma then back to Sam. "No, not this time. What made you ask that?"

"Aw, I heard on the news earlier that some bloke over in Cunnamulla died from a spider bite. Funnel web, I think they said. Don't know much about them, but I don't like them anyway. Then some woman yesterday ended up in critical condition from some spider bite. Happened pretty quickly."

"Where was that?"

"Down in Canberra or thereabouts. Anyway, so what happened to make you yell out? You sure you're ok?"

John's expression had darkened. What Sam had told him was disturbing. He looked up to Sam's face and met his eyes. "Yea, I'm fine now. Just had a bit of a scare. Sam did they say what that thing looks like?"

Sam cleared his throat, looking down in thought and back up to him. "Said it was big and black. Didn't quite get it all."

"Hmm. Well, mate, what I saw coming at me on the rake handle was big and black; and it was definitely a spider. Biggest one I ever seen."

Sam's eyes widened a bit. "Really? You don't say?"

John nodded his head. "That's what made me yell out."

"Where'd ya see it?"

John pointed to the front bushes.

"If I were you, I'd stay away from that spot. Keep your doors and windows shut. If that was a funnel web you saw, you don't want it getting inside. From what they said, it can make a pretty nasty bite and worse. Well, gotta get back to the old lady. She's got some errands for me to run. Talk to ya later. Be careful."

John and Norma waved as he left. "Yea, you too, Sam. Thanks for the info."

As the two turned to go inside the house, John's expression remained on the dark side. Now what was he going to do? He couldn't stop living or his chores just because of some multi-legged critter. He was adamant about not letting something like that run his life or his schedule. He'd figure out a way to avoid that trouble again.

#

December 5, Canberra, New South Wales

There wasn't much else to do right now as most of the loose items were picked up and put away. Sandy's room was straightened out and looked ideally neat, clean, and definitely a girl's room. There were pink curtains with a few pictures of Hello Kitty on them, a couple of small pink teddy bears and a doll on the bed, and a play makeup kit on her small dresser that had light bulbs around its small mirror. Two windows let the daylight in to brighten up the room. She'd have to be at work in two and a half hours.

Before she could go down and turn off the downstairs TV, the phone rang. It was Emily from the church women's group.

"Hi, there girl, what's up?" Tabitha was always cheerful on the phone. She and Emily were good friends.

"Hey there, thought I'd ask to see if you want to come over tomorrow night for a little session at my house. We're going to discuss having a ladies night out dinner at the church as a fundraiser for helping homeless children out there."

The Ingrams belonged to the New Hope Baptist Church on the other side of the city. She loved the minister and the people there who returned the feelings back to her and her family. They also reached out to people who might be in need of help. They were a close-knit very loving family.

Tabitha brushed her hair back with her hand. "Sure, sounds like a good cause. What time?"

"About 7:30. Refreshments and non-alcoholic drinks on me. Can you make it?"

"Sure. I'll be there. Can I bring anything, chips and dip, something like that?"

"No, I'll have that here, luv. Just bring yourself and any ideas you might have."

"Ok, I'll be there. Gotta finish up here and then get a couple of hours in at work."

"Thought this was your day off?" Emily asked curiously.

"Well it was. Kathy called me to help if I could do it. Short-handed, you know. I agreed to put in three hours."

"Alright, then, luv. I won't hold you up. Have fun at work and see you tomorrow night. Say hi to Peter and Sandy for me." Tabitha promised she would and after hanging up, turned to go back downstairs.

5

December 5, Sydney, New South Wale-3:00pm

The whistle blew which meant the workday was over. Men and women lined up to punch out, tired and eager to get home after the usual grueling day. Making parts for engines was not the most glamorous job in the world, but for Rodney Johnson, the metalworker, it was a job and he was glad to have it. It paid well and the bennies were better than average, so he had no complaints. But still, he was always glad when it was time to go home.

The drive each way took him only about a half hour. He lived 50 kilometers or about 31 miles from work, down in Wollongong, close to the coast. Divorced and a father of three, Rodney lived alone now in a small house outside of town with only his two cats to keep him company. Despite his amicable visitation arrangements with his kids with him being the non-custodial parent, he was still lonely. Fortunately for the entire family, it was not a messy divorce. They were friendly enough. But they just couldn't live together anymore.

When he arrived home, he did the usual things: got the mail and checked it, and threw off his shoes to relax. After that, he checked the cat dishes for food and water and the litter box. He saw Friskie come running out of one of the rooms.

"Hey there, boy, what's up there matey, eh?" Oddly, the cat just kept running by him and disappeared around a corner into another room. It always met him when he arrived home and would nuzzle his leg and allow Rodney to pet him. That was practically written in stone. This was the first time he had done just the opposite. Rod stood up with a genuine look of concern on his face. He knew something had spooked his cat, but couldn't imagine what. He was an indoor cat. There was nothing in here that should scare him. Ah, maybe he's just catnapping, he thought to himself. He went to the kitchen, tapped into the refrigerator for a beer, returned to the living room and sat on the sofa to relax for a few minutes and unwind.

After a few minutes of sipping his beer and listening to the voices on the TV, he started wondering where his other male cat, Max, was.

"Max, hey Max, where are ya, ya little rascal? Come to papa. Papa's home." He figured that calling out to him might bring him around.

He went from room to room looking for the black cat that was actually more of a "good luck" pet for him than anything else, despite his entirely black fur. Rod was never superstitious anyway. To him, black cats and walking under ladders was only a myth or pure folklore. He never took what he considered such nonsense seriously.

When he entered his bedroom, at first he saw only the usual display of his unmade bed and the few disarrayed items on his bureau. He didn't want to let his house get too messy because he didn't want to give the wrong impression to his ex-wife that he couldn't take care of his own home. That could have an effect on the weekend visits from his kids. Being the non-custodial parent, he had to be careful about that.

As he looked around, he kept calling out for Max. "Hmm, strange," he muttered out loud. It was not like Max to not run to him and rub himself against Rod's lower legs as a sign of affection and a kind of "glad you're finally home, daddy" type of response. Rod began to feel some concern. Had the cat gotten out? He didn't see him anywhere.

He couldn't understand it because the windows were all closed. The door to the basement was closed so he couldn't have gone down there. But he decided to check there anyway.

A few minutes later he came back upstairs, more perplexed than ever. Where in tarnations had Max gone? Friskie came up to him and rubbed briefly against his lower legs. "Where's your brother, eh matey?" he asked the cat without expecting any kind of response to that. "Where is he? Damn, I wish you could talk." The cat looked up at him as if to say, "Yeah, me too."

When Rodney walked into the living room, he checked around, and under the chairs and sofa. He turned on the ceiling light to decrease some of the shadows in the room. As he went around and checked the back of the sofa, he thought he saw something sticking out from under it. It looked like the tip of something but he couldn't be sure what it was.

He slid the couch forward, but found that something seemed to hinder its movement. He looked back down to the back of it and saw part of a furry black leg. At that very moment, as his jaw dropped, he felt as if his heart dropped all the way down to the floor.

"No," he muttered, "No, no, no, no, no no, Max!" The adrenaline suddenly kicked in and with an increased strength he flipped the sofa over until it was upside down. There on the floor in front of him was his beloved Max. He was stiff as a board, with his tongue lolling out and eyes glazed over looking at empty nothingness.

Rodney dropped to the floor, the shock temporarily keeping the inevitable tears at bay. He looked at his dead cat wondering what happened, why it happened, and what could have killed him. At his last checkup, the vet gave him a clean bill of health. That was only two months ago. There was no diagnosis of any kind of illness, no feline leukemia, or anything else that can afflict cats. Was there a snake in the house? In his search for Max, he hadn't seen any. He decided he needed to find out what killed his Max. As he picked the body up to bring it to the vet, he failed to notice something black squeeze itself down and quickly disappear between the slats of a heating vent on the floor in the corner of the room.

#

Two days before at Sydney Memorial Hospital, the nurse had first spoken with a Dr. Thomas Wilkinson, an entomologist and arachnologist with the Department of Entomology at UA, then she transferred the call to Dr. Williamson. Based on what he told him, the doctor came up with his unofficial diagnosis of what Ken Walker had most likely died of. He basically confirmed what Dr. Mayberry from the Department of Parks and Wildlife had said on television. Ken Walker had died of envenomation from the Sydney Funnel Web spider. So the doctor, once he found out the culprit and all the other information put together, then made his official diagnosis for the records. It was not something he looked forward to passing on, but knew he had to do. It didn't take long for word to spread throughout the hospital.

6

December 5, University of Sydney, New South Wales

Mary Welling, PhD and arachnologist, sat at her bench examining the species of Arachnida called the green jumping spider, which she knew as *Mopsus mormom*. Although there were 5,000 or more species of jumping spiders, she'd always been particularly interested in this one member of this family of Salticidae. It was the largest sized jumping spider in Australia and had been known to cannibalize its own kind.

As she studied the dead specimen on her lab table with her tweezers, the door to the lab opened and a familiar voice rang out through the cool air. Her longtime friend and colleague, Tom Wilkinson came in whistling. It sounded like he was in a cheerful mood. Or was he? Sometimes he whistled when he was deep in thought.

"Tom, that you?" Mary asked.

"Yep. In between classes right now. Have to give a lecture this afternoon on Dermatobia hominis. Ought to be fun I'd say. Should rightly freak a couple of the students out I predict."

Mary turned and looked up at him as he approached from behind. "Well, hey, what do you expect? Not everyone finds the human botfly exactly an interesting subject, ya know."

He put his hand on her back and gently caressed it up and down. "You're right. Not everyone does." He bent down and put his face close to hers. "But one subject I do find extremely fascinating to the most extreme."

She turned her face to his until they almost touched. "Ah, I know what that is: the ten-eyed dung beetle." He laughed at the tease and creative name.

"That's a good one, luv. Have to remember that. No, this is what I find fascinating." And he kissed her, expecting and getting one in full return.

They'd been dating for a couple of years now. Both had previous bad relationships involving cheating and misrepresentations. Mary had suffered also from some physical abuse from her ex while Thomas had endured a perpetually increasing problem of greed and selfishness from his ex. After their subsequent divorces, they each took their time finding companionship. Eventually, they got to know each other at the school and in the lab. In time, they knew each other well enough to be confident that no similar previous problems would occur between the two of them. Now Thomas believed he was in love with her, but wasn't so sure about how she felt about him. He decided to wait a little longer before he would approach the subject of feelings and potential commitment. He wanted to be extra careful and not spook her.

After he pulled away, he looked down at what she was examining.

"So what are we looking at today?" Although he was also an arachnologist, he couldn't tell for sure what he was looking at because she had the thing in pieces on her insectiboard, is what she called it.

She told him.

"Mopsus mormom. Interesting spider. I think all the jumping spiders are." He stood up and with hands in his pockets looked straight ahead of him, the vanished smile replaced by a look of concern.

She continued to keep her eyes on him, knowing him better than he could have imagined.

"Alright, sweetheart, spill it."

He looked back down at her. "Spill it? What are you..." Then he realized. He had forgotten how he unwittingly always signaled nonverbally when something bothered or concerned him. Somehow Mary could always sense or see this in him. He might as well wave a huge flag in front of her with the words, "Trouble on the forefront". He sighed and returned her look. His voice deepened a bit with the seriousness of his concern.

"Heard the latest news?" he asked her.

"News? Afraid not, my love. I've been here all morning. Chose not to turn the radio on so I wouldn't be distracted. No classes today."

He then told her about Ken Walker.

#

December 5, Canberra, New South Wales

With her simple chores completed upstairs and having finished on the phone with Emily, Tabitha headed back downstairs to turn the TV off. Looks like she'd have a little down time before heading off to the restaurant.

It was close to 11:00 am. After turning the television off, she looked through the one window where the sun came in, brightening up the usually dim room. There was a table across the dryer. Underneath that table was an old wooden box she kept for storing some old items. The box was actually handed down to her from her grandparents which made it an heirloom as far as she was concerned and there would be no plans to get rid of it, despite its age and less than attractive appearance. It was out of sight and not in the way of anything, so most of the time it remained out of mind for her. Once a week when she vacuumed the room of its always quickly-accumulating dust, she'd see it and would make sure she cleaned all the way around it. Dusting the top of it would round out her cleaning tasks down here.

Behind her there was silent movement on the floor. She found one of her panties on the floor near the box. Apparently it unknowingly to her had dropped on the floor when she removed the clothes from the dryer earlier.

"Damn, I hate when that happens," she muttered out loud to herself.

She bent down to pick up the panty which was up against the bottom of the box. As her hand grabbed it, she felt a sudden pain on the top of her right hand.

"Ow!" she yelled out, pulling her hand back with lightning speed. What the hell was that? "Oh shit!" She looked at her hand noticing very small holes close together. There was a tiny amount of blood. Did she poke herself to a nail that may have been sticking out from the box? Initially she thought that may be the case. When she looked at the bottom of the box while holding her hand, she didn't see any nail sticking out. Try as hard as she did, she saw nothing down there; until she looked to the left side of the box. There she saw something that might have given someone with a weak heart a heart attack. It was huge, black and was reared onto its hind legs in a frightening display of pure threat. It was partially hidden in the shadow created by the box. Yet she could see what appeared to be two large fangs curving downward. Her jaw dropped as her hand pain increased. The sight of it prevented her temporarily from seeing the quick swelling and reddening of her hand.

"Oh my God," she muttered and then grimaced. She stepped back in horror and felt another sudden pain in the area just above the left Achilles tendon. She screamed. "What the hell is happening here?" she yelled out.

She started to feel dizzy and became wobbly on her feet. Without realizing it, her feet brought her back a step again and there was another shot of lightning bolt pain just above her left foot. With whatever bearings she had, she turned and backed away from the area, watching the two large black spiders appearing to face her now from each side of the machine area.

She had no idea where they came from or what they were doing down here. They had never had a spider problem down here before; in fact, they never had any kind of a bug problem because she kept the area spotless and sprayed just for good measure. As she held her hand and started heading toward the stairs, she briefly glanced ahead and saw the open door. Initially it didn't really register with her until now. They had come through it, out of the darkness.

The pain in her hand was tremendous and the same pain was increasing in her left Achilles area. Scrambling for the stairs, she started to climb up but with increased difficulty, even holding onto the rails. Taking one step at a time, she felt her legs weighed a ton each and she could barely lift them. The sweat was literally pouring off of her and she could now feel numbness and tingling around her mouth. Every move she made now was a struggle. Whatever was inside of her was working very quickly. She was scared like never before but was determined to get to that phone upstairs. There was no way she was going to try and use the phone down here with those things here, whatever they were. She knew they were spiders but didn't know the kind. To her, they all looked alike, except that these were the biggest she'd ever seen.

As she slowly took each step upward, she found herself breathing more heavily. In fact, her breathing became more difficult with each minute that passed. Soon she started seeing double of everything and felt delirium creep in. She had to get to the phone upstairs. As she took another step up, her dizziness continued to increase along with her pain. For at least a couple of minutes, she found herself unable to take another step as the pain became unbearable and the numbness made her feel like she had no mouth. What started coming out of it were more like loud moans rather than screams. Now the entirety of both her legs felt they were on fire.

"Dear Lord, please help," she tried to mutter but couldn't quite get it out. Waves of nausea swept over her as her dizziness, delirium, and double vision came to a head within minutes. She was stuck in the middle of the stairs trying to hold on without being able to move. Her terror of what was happening to her made her heart beat even faster than it was. The feeling of impending doom overpowered her. The thought of dying here alone and never having the chance to say goodbye to her family was equally terrifying.

Determined to make it to the top, she fought for all she was worth. Despite her arms feeling like they weighed a ton, she grabbed each step and did her best to pull herself up using her legs at the same time to give herself some measure of boost. When she looked up, the doorway looked a long way off, yet it was actually only a few feet away. Then she felt another sharp pain, this time on the back of her right thigh, then another. She had been unable to feel anything crawling up the back of her legs as she tried to climb up the stairs. Unable to feel anything but agonizing pain, she was bitten again on her right arm. The pain, in her mind, was worse than that of childbirth. As the huge amount of venom in her body was quickly destroying her organs and flesh, moving became an almost impossible task. Her screams of pain lessened into little more than whimpers of extreme agony as her life quickly approached its ending. There would be no help for her and she started seeing flashes of her life in her mind.

Minutes ticked by, and she had, with painstaking slowness managed to drag herself up only about three steps. Her breathing was more labored and her pain now involved her entire body. She could barely keep her eyes open as they started rolling upwards. She wanted to scream as loud as she could, but her breathing difficulty made that nearly impossible. Then she was hit with an additional problem.

Her legs started spasming and convulsing but more severely in her left leg. The muscles in her left thigh were severely rippling and undulating causing her more excruciating pain. She screamed this time, despite the breathing difficulties. At this point she had lost all voluntary control of her movements. Her bodily functions were gone and her bladder released all of its contents. The venom had taken her over completely, destroying the inside of her and her normal functioning. No longer was she able to drag herself any further up. This was when she knew. She'd never see her loving little girl again or her beloved husband. The tears flowed out of her tormented eyes as she lost consciousness. Her life was ending here on the stairs.

Before her soul left her body, a small fragment of her cognitive awareness remained for a short time, lagging behind the exiting of her life as if to stall the inevitable. Her mind envisioned a little girl standing beside her parents when they lived down in Melbourne, then as a high school teenager and some of the friends she had, her fiancé and soon to be husband ten years ago, and the death of her father. Her mouth closed as the numbness and tingling spread to other parts of her face. She lost all ability to move or obey any commands from her brain which was now devoid of nearly all function. "I love you Sandy. I love you Peter," she would have wanted to say. Her body gave a final death twitch, her muscles were now totally limp. One last gasp of death emitted from her mouth as she quickly now descended into blackness with a bright light at its end.

Gravity took over. Her body collapsed and then fell down the stairs landing face up at the bottom. She felt nothing. With open, now sightless eyes, she lay there but not alone. Her body was quickly covered by hundreds of the creatures which emerged from the surrounding dark areas.

7

December 5, Canberra, New South Wales

At 1:30pm, the phone rang but there was no answer. Kathy Beasley, Tabitha's boss, was concerned because it was completely unlike Tabitha not to call if she was going to be late for any reason, let alone not show up at all. She tried three times without success. Then she looked up and found her cell phone number and tried that. To her dismay, her phone went right to voice mail. Definitely not a good sign because Tabitha had told her once that she always turned on her cell phone right before she left the house for any reason. At home she always used her home phone. So based on that, Kathy figured she must still be at home, yet she was not answering. Something was wrong.

As she looked through the window of her office at her workers and the few customers that were there, she was struggling to decide whether or not she should go and check on her. She decided to try phoning her one more time and if no luck, she'd try to find her. When her further phone attempts ended with the same results, she got up and informed the lead waitress, Shirley, that she'd be leaving for a while to check on something important. She didn't feel the need to explain what that was. When Shirley nodded and said she'd keep things running, Kathy said she'd return soon and left.

Fifteen minutes later, she arrived at the Ingrams' and parked in the driveway beside Tabitha's car. Just the fact that her car was still there told her she was still home, and the fact that she hadn't answered the phone was a huge red flag for her. Suddenly she felt the feeling in her stomach of fear and increasing apprehension. It wasn't so much that she knew something was wrong: it was more of a *sensation* that something was wrong. A gut feeling. Rarely did she ignore something like that because it didn't occur very often.

Looking at the outside front of the two story home, she didn't notice anything out of the ordinary. The front door was closed. The small flower gardens that complemented each side of the front door along with the neatly mowed and well-kept lawn made the home attractive in appearance. It was a beautiful home, although Kathy had never been inside. Even though she was not a close friend to Tabitha, still she considered herself a friend to her because she cared about her employees. She hadn't wanted to get too close to any of them out of fear of losing her objectivity in supervising them at work. But she knew that Tabitha was nearly the most reliable employee she had ever supervised.

Getting out of her car, she walked to the front door and pressed the doorbell. Waiting anxiously and hoping Tabitha would answer, it was hard for her to not just burst through the door and call out to her. After a minute went by and there was no response either verbally or at the door itself, she tried the door. It was locked. 'Damn,' she thought. She rang the bell numerous times rapidly but her only response once again was no response.

Walking quickly around to the back to see if there was another way in or if her worker just happened to be back there for some reason, she found one of the two back doors but no sign of Tabitha. There was an upper back door with stairs leading up to it, which she figured led to the kitchen area. The lower door she assumed led into the basement or lower living area, she wasn't sure. She had no idea what she would find but hoped it would be open so she could at least gain entry and see if maybe Tabitha had an accident and couldn't get to the phone or maybe got sick and passed out. She had to find out. By this time, the" butterflies" in her stomach seemed to increase in number.

She decided to try the upper door first because the upper floors seemed to be the most likely place to find her if she was here. It was locked, so she went back down to the yard and to the other door. To her surprise, it opened when she turned the knob. 'Hallelujah,' she said to herself.

Opening it slowly, she descended the few steps ignoring the webbing that was brushing by her. At the bottom and through another door, her eyes were met by a neat-looking room that indicated it was not a living area. Straight ahead and also to her right were white plastered walls. The room was semi-dim, with only a couple of regular light bulbs on the ceiling lighting it up and some daylight coming through the small window. She looked to her left and saw an open doorway which led into the main room, and at the opposite end of the room were the washer and dryer. Clearly this was the Ingram's laundry area.

She called out loudly to Tabitha, identifying herself as she slowly walked to that doorway. She hated going into someone else's house without invitation because it made her feel like an intruder. Only an eerie silence met her calls. Just like the doorbell and the phone. Fear suddenly took hold of her and she felt the hairs stand up on the back of her neck. What if there was a *real* intruder and he was still in the house? What kind of danger would that place her in? She wasn't sure if she should proceed further. Now she *knew* something was certainly wrong. She just didn't know what.

Her decision was made. She would go only into that room but would not go upstairs. If she didn't find her down here, she'd return back outside and call the police on her cell. Slowly and carefully she walked to the doorway, looking through it. Nothing ahead of her. To her right was where the sight caused her jaw to drop, her eyes to widen suddenly. There on the floor at the bottom of a staircase was Tabitha.

"Tabitha, oh my God, Tabitha!" She started walking quickly toward her, realizing she was at the very least unconscious if not worse. As she started bending down to see if she was still alive, her eyes got wider and she stepped back in such horror that she couldn't quite get a scream out.

There on her neck and chest were two large black spiders, the likes of which she'd never seen before. Tarantulas? She didn't know. As she backed through the doorway from which she came through, she almost couldn't take her eyes off the horror she had just witnessed. Did those things kill her? In her mind, it certainly looked like it. Or did she just fall down the stairs? Because the sight was so shocking to unexpectedly confront, she was not able to see the huge red swelling of her right hand or on her lowermost left leg.

Kathy quickly turned and ran back outside from where she'd come. Dialing the local emergency number, she reported what she'd seen and her location. An ambulance and police were quickly dispatched to the home. Because of the spiders she saw, an entomologist who knew about spiders also was called to assess the creatures she had seen. Special precautions were issued to the first responders. She waited there in the front yard to meet them, calling her restaurant to inform them she wouldn't be in the rest of the day due to an emergency. Now was not the time to break the news to them, especially on the phone.

#

December 6, Sydney, New South Wales

In the morning, Rodney brought his beloved Max to the vet's office. Even though the cat was dead, he hadn't been sick beforehand. There was nothing while he was alive to suggest that anything was wrong with it. He couldn't understand it and felt the powerful need to find out what could have killed it. Even though, to some people, it was just a cat it was still a part of him, just as a close family member would be. He loved Max and he knew that the cat had loved him back. Although the cat couldn't tell him that and skeptics would claim that cats can't love anybody because they're animals, he didn't buy that. He knew and *believed.* Therefore he owed it to Max and to himself to find out.

The veterinarian readily agreed to do the necropsy, but it would have to wait a couple of hours because of a couple of scheduled patients she had to see, including a German shepherd with a gum problem and a

Norwegian Elkhound which seemed to have some kind of gastric disorder. But she promised Rod that she'd get to the cat today, and that he could wait or come back later. If he chose to return later, the doctor advised him that she'd have a staff member call to inform him that the results were ready. Rodney told her he'd have to go to work right now but he'd check with her later and would be back right after work at 3pm. With that arrangement, Rodney left for his job at the plant, with apprehension sticking at the back of his mind about what the results would tell him. He wouldn't quite be the happy, cheerful worker he normally was today. If he could, he would have taken bereavement leave. Seeing as employers don't allow bereavement leave for animals passed away, he went in without complaint.

8

December 6, University of Sydney, New South Wales

Although Mary Welling was disturbed by the news yesterday, something like that wasn't unheard of in Australia. The things could be deadly but because of modern, new and improved treatment methods and the availability of anti-venom for the funnel web, most victims were able to get the proper treatment well within the necessary time frame for complete recovery. Unfortunately for Ken Walker, she realized as the others had, he had waited too long to call for help which ushered in his eventual demise.

Her class wouldn't start for another fifteen minutes. She had about ten students in her entomology class, which was about average. Not a lot of people enjoyed the scientific study of bugs and other multi-legged creatures because it wasn't just about book-studying them. They actually had a lab to go with the class where they had to handle and dissect them. This included the larger arachnids such as spiders. Most college students were creeped out by these creepers. On the other hand, most students here who took the class enjoyed this branch of science with many going on to eventually become entomologists or other scientists in their own right.

Her desk was on the messy side, but she decided she could clean it up later. With ten minutes to go, she decided to grab a coffee and head on over to the classroom. Her office was very small, so she appreciated that much more the spaciousness of the classroom whenever she went there.

With coffee in hand in her traveling mug, she headed toward the stairs leading to the classroom. Before she could start ascending, she heard a voice behind her.

"Hey Mary, got a minute?" It was Dean John Minson, the head of the biological science department.

Mary turned and smiled. "Hey! What's up John? My class doesn't start for another seven or eight minutes. What can I do for you?"

The dean could fit, for some, stereotypical appearing for a man of his position: short and thin, bald, and with horn-rimmed glasses. All in all, he was pretty decent for a dean and treated everyone fairly, including his staff.

"Just thought I'd let you know. I don't know if you heard. Heard it on the news just now. Had a death here in Canberra. Suspected spider bite. Actually bites, I should say."

Mary looked surprised. "Really? Here in town?"

"You got it. It's not official yet. The media let loose its loose lips and decided before the coroner what killed the woman. She was a mother of a young daughter who was supposed to report for work not long after the incident."

"You said bites, John. How do they know it's a spider bite and that it's more than one if the autopsy hasn't been completed yet?"

"The witness, a woman who happened to be her boss who found her body on the floor inside her room. She found two large black spiders sitting on top of her. From what I heard, the paramedics saw a grossly swollen right hand and huge swelling on her left lower leg.

"Not only that, but now that's come out, reports from all over the city and even outside the city are coming in about these things coming out and into where they shouldn't be. People are really becoming scared now. Could we be having an Arachnophobia situation here, non-Hollywood style?"

Mary was surprised. This was the most bizarre thing she'd ever heard. Yet despite that, her gut feeling was that it was true, despite it being a media "diagnosis".

"Have the spiders been identified as to genus and species?"

The dean shook his head. "No, not yet. I'm no spider expert like you, but it sounds to me sort of maybe, wolf or funnel webs. I don't know for sure, but if I hear something else I'll let you know."

Mary looked at him with concern. "Ok. Thanks John. I'd appreciate that. I wouldn't go so far as to think this is the movie come to life. Don't want that. Can you imagine the panic that might start? That's the last thing we need right now."

"Yea, you're right." Then he shook his head.

"What a tragedy. That poor young girl is now without a mother. Her dad was notified and is with her now. Well, I'll let you go. See ya later." With that, he turned and headed down the hall to his office.

That's two in two days, she thought to herself. Quickly assessing the facts given to her, she began to rule out Wolf spiders in her mind. According to what the dean said, both spiders were black. Many wolf spiders are not but may be gray or have yellowish markings. In addition, they are usually not known to go into people's homes but prefer woodlands, shrub lands, or wet coastal forests. Whereas the Sydney funnel webs are a shiny black and can wander into or become trapped in houses. They also don't jump onto or chase people. She knew that the Brazilian wandering spider or banana spider could jump onto a person before biting, but not the funnel web. So why were these two spiders on the victim, if what John said was true? From the visible symptoms of swelling, the cause could have been from either type of spider. Yet the woman was dead.

But there was another difference. Wolf spider symptoms are relatively minor and almost never cause death. But the Sydney funnel web can certainly be deadly, as was unfortunately proven by Ken Walker. She'd never heard of someone dying from the Wolf spider. In her mind, unless she was given more information to disprove what she believed at the moment, her conclusion would stand. Could there be a Sydney Funnel Web spider problem brewing? She had no more time to figure that out. There would be time for that later. Now she had to get to the classroom before her students started wondering if there was going to be a class.

December 6, Sydney, New South Wales, late afternoon

Rodney had known Dr. Louise Ellen Binder for several years. She was a very good veterinarian and had treated his cats previously for shots and immunizations. There was one time he thought that Friskie may have developed feline leukemia and he was pretty much stressed out over it. When he brought her in to the vet office that morning two years ago, Dr. Binder examined her very carefully and tested her. She considered the animals she treated just as important not only as individuals, but as patients as well, just as any good doctor for humans would. There was no end for her love of animals and the work she did with her patients was evidence of that.

In Friskie's case, it was a huge relief to Rodney that Friskie did not have leukemia but merely a cold virus, which was relatively mild and she would eventually get over it.

When Rodney returned at 3:50 that afternoon, he had been a little anxious to find out what the doctor discovered. Despite his emotional upset over the loss of his cat, he couldn't take off from work for bereavement reasons and there was nothing he could do anyway. Besides, he had figured working might keep his mind off what happened.

The vet assistant had him wait in the waiting room until the doctor could get to him. In a few minutes she came out.

"Hi Rod, sorry to keep you waiting."

"Hi Doc. What 'cha got for me?"

He noticed her voice had sounded pleasant enough; yet there was a slight undertone to it that kind of alerted him that the news might not be all that he would have expected.

"C'mon back here to my office."

'Uh oh,' he said to himself. 'That doesn't sound good.'

After he was seated in her office and she sat behind her desk, she pulled out some papers and photographs. He noticed her pleasant smile change into a look of concern as she looked directly at him.

"Rod, before I get into this, let me ask you: did you ever have your home exterminated or have it examined by pest control?"

The question took Rodney by surprise. "Uh, no. Never had a reason to. Why?"

"Well, let me tell you. I did a pretty thorough necropsy on Max. By the way, I'm so sorry about your loss. I feel bad about this, so this isn't the easiest thing for me to have to report to you. But you need to know.

"Anyway, as I said, the necropsy was pretty thorough because initially I couldn't find anything wrong that could have killed him. His organs appeared fine, he appeared healthy and well fed. None of his systems showed any signs of malignancies or other growths. I saw no abnormalities. That includes examination of the brain. Although I hadn't shaved off all of his fur but only those areas I would surgically examine initially, when I couldn't find anything on the initial exam, I shaved off the rest of his fur, from his face down and including his tail. There was something amiss that I figured could involve a clue hidden by the fur."

"Doc, what does the question you asked about pest control have to do with this?" Rodney started feeling some tension in his stomach. He knew she wouldn't have asked that unless there was something to it.

"I'm getting to that. Let me give you the facts leading up to it so you'll understand better. When I examined Max more thoroughly, his skin now exposed, I found what looked like two little puncture holes around the left neck area. They definitely would have been invisible under the fur."

Rodney's jaw dropped. What the hell? He sat forward. "Puncture holes?" he asked, as if he wanted to make sure he heard her correctly.

"That's right. What *looked* like puncture holes. I thought that pretty strange. After making sure they weren't merely birth marks or other natural anomalies, my conclusion was that they were. From what, I don't know."

"Rats maybe? Or mice?" Rodney asked with increasing anxiety. He hated rodents with a passion to the point where he was almost afraid of them. "I've never seen them around anywhere my place. If I did or saw any signs of their presence, like droppings, I would have been on the horn faster than you can shake a stick."

Dr. Binder shook her head. "No, these were not rodent markings. They were from something but not from any rodent. Rodents have incisors which make different size and shaped puncture marks than these. These were from something smaller and were rounder in appearance."

"What about bats?" Rodney asked, thinking about it all of a sudden.

"Seen any in your house, attic, or basement recently? Or ever?"

Rodney frowned, shaking his head. "No, can't say that I have."

"Do you know of any bats anywhere in your area or close to it? Or have been told by people of bats they saw in the area?"

"No, no one ever told me they saw them anywhere, not even at night."

"Although those marks *could* have been made by a bat, based on what you told me, I think it'll be unlikely that the tests would indicate that.

"Anyway, based on that, the tests I'm talking about would be on the blood and tissues. I won't get the results for a couple of days. However, I do suspect that those marks had something to do with the cat's death. I won't know for sure until I get the results. I'm suspecting at this point that he didn't die a natural death."

"You mean something killed him?"

Binder nodded. "That's what I'm thinking. But I can't give the official findings for the report until I get those results. And I know you'll want to know as soon as possible. So I'll give you a call. In fact, I sent them with requests to expedite as soon as possible due to a life and death situation. Might have been a bit of an exaggeration, but then maybe not. I rarely put that in there, so it just might catch their attention and get them going on it right away."

Rodney looked away, deep in thought. This was certainly disturbing, but he was confident that Lou Ellen did the right thing. Although he was anxious to find out about Max's killer, he understood that the waiting would have to occur for the results.

"Ok, I appreciate it, Doc. I'll certainly want to find out as soon as you can get back to me about it."

"You know I will, Rod. In the meantime, relax and know this matter is in good hands. They will get back to me asap and I'll do the same in turn for you. I'm as anxious to find out as you are. I've not seen anything like this in any of my patients, I have to tell you. And a word of caution: I don't mean to scare you but be wary of anything in your house that you see that shouldn't be there. I know that sounds kinda crazy. But that's only because something in your house killed Max. It may not be necessarily harmful to you, however. But take precautions anyway. Just to be on the safe side. Any more questions for me?"

"No, I don't think so, Doc." He thanked her as he stood along with her and they shook hands. "Thanks so much for doing this," he added. "I appreciate this."

"Hey, anytime, Rod. Like I said, I want to find out the results also as bad as you do. He was your cat and he was my patient. So I guess we both have a stake in this, eh?"

With pleasant goodbyes and the start of the tense waiting, Rodney left the vet's office with his mind now going a mile a minute. *Something in my house?* Well if that doesn't sound like something from a horror movie. Looks like he had some work to do when he got home.

9

December 8, Sydney, New South Wales

Dr. Binder hadn't told Rodney everything because she wasn't one hundred percent sure of what she believed was true. And she didn't want to scare Rodney unnecessarily, having just given him a mild safety warning.

She knew those puncture marks weren't from any bat. They *could* have been had there been some around; more likely by a rabid one at that. But bats weren't endemic to their local area. She had known them to be further west and south than Sydney. So it had to be something else. She was thinking of something but she'd have to do some research on her findings and see if she could come up with something else before she contacted any experts. She knew who to contact if she needed to.

After she finished with her last patient of the day, a Chihuahua with a mild condition of eczema, she finished her reports and then quickly checked her computer out of great curiosity to see if she could quickly find a possibility of what she was thinking.

Going to the Google search engine, she typed in the information she wanted to explore. It brought her to the page she wanted, and she clicked on one of the many listings. A detailed page appeared on her screen. She then looked up medical symptoms and other related information as well as taking a very close look at particular close up pictures. What she was seeing was pretty frightening. She saw an image of what could have made those puncture marks on Max. Reading the symptoms of toxicity, she realized that this was only a possibility, not a certainty. But it was worth looking into further.

Yet what she had read about it in detail left a gap as to the certainty of it being a possible culprit. The information stated that dogs, cats, and various other mammals seemed to be resistant to its venom. Yet, this cat had died. Was it from the funnel web spider venom, and if so why wasn't it resistant to it?

Knowing that, she anticipated that the blood test results would likely provide her with the critical information she needed to come to a final conclusion of Max's death. She looked more closely at the close-up images. Although she loved animals, spiders were not at the top of her favorites list. What she saw was frightening. And she knew it was endemic to their very area and it went into houses. Reading about it only increased her concern and anxiety about the case. She knew what she had to do but it would have to wait until the tests came back. She'd call the lab tomorrow and see if they could tell her anything. One thing she wouldn't do was alarm someone prematurely, especially if she was wrong. At the same time, she didn't want to wait too long either. Tomorrow would be the kicker. She did warn Rodney to be on the lookout for anything out of the ordinary in his home. Bearing that in mind, it gave her some solace. With that, she turned off the computer and gathered her things for leaving. Tomorrow would be another but very important day.

#

December 8, University of Sydney, late afternoon

It was her last class of the day and Mary Welling saw it was full, which she was always glad about. It gave her the positive feeling that the students enjoyed her class and chose to be there rather than miss it. It ran from 4pm to 5:15pm today. Other class days were at earlier times. Today's discussion would be about the life cycles of two of the most prevalent flying insects on the planet: flies and mosquitoes. While most students would laugh at the idea of other students actually studying about these lowly, hated creatures of the air, entomology students seemed to be a different breed of student all their own. The only people on planet earth who seemed to perceive that roles for these creatures actually existed in ecosystems were entomologists and biologists. Everyone else considered them insects from hell, reminiscent of the devil flies in the movie, *The Amityville Horror.*

"Ok, good afternoon everyone. I hope everyone read up on chapters 15 and 18 of the text. We're going to discuss today one of sciences' most magnanimous subjects: the fly. Before we begin, does anyone have any questions about anything we have discussed up to this point?"

Mary looked at the students and saw a hand go up. "Yes, Paul."

"Dr. Welling, I know that this isn't part of this discussion today but I was wondering if you heard about the latest funnel web invasion in the city?"

Some of the other students quickly turned their heads to look at him, surprised and somewhat fearful of the question. If Paul was joking, they didn't find his joke a bit funny. A couple of the other students who had heard the same thing expressed that out loud. Soon voices multiplied within the student area.

"Alright, let's settle down if you will." Her eyes refocused on Paul.

"Paul, where did you hear that?"

"Well, word is going around the school. How that started I don't know. Some think it's a joke and rumor that someone started to crank people up. Others believe it's for real. Wondering have *you* heard anything about that?"

Mary sighed. *'Well, I opened that Pandora's box asking for questions,'* she thought to herself. She had to address this, especially if something like that was going around the school. What better place to quell the potential panic like the entomology department?

All the students had their eyes glued to her as they waited for what she would say. If not all of them had cared to ask that question, now they were all interested in the answer.

She leaned against the clean blackboard area with her arms crossed with the intentions of squashing this rumor before it spread anymore, if what Paul said was true.

"Ok, I see this is an issue that won't be quickly resolved talking about flies. So let me see if I can set your minds at ease at least for the moment. First of all, I don't believe that there has been an *invasion*. Paul, on what basis do you consider this problem an invasion?"

All eyes turned to Paul. "They're saying that three people have already died from those spiders within a week's time. Right in their own homes."

"Is that all? Just three spiders?" she challenged him.

"Um, actually no. On one of them, the newspaper said two spiders were found on the woman's body."

Suddenly some of the students were talking to each other commenting on Paul's reply. Mary was surprised at that because she hadn't read or heard about it. Yet.

"When did that come out?" she asked Paul.

"This morning's Herald." That was the paper she hadn't read. Normally she read the paper each morning, but because she had overslept and was in a rush to complete her morning breakfast, cleanup and getting to work, she hadn't had time to see it.

Mary looked down at the floor in thought. She was concerned now but wanted to minimize the students seeing that on her face. They were alarmed about it enough without her contribution to the potential panic.

Looking back up at them, she took a deep breath and let it out before beginning her serious attempt to calm the issue here in the classroom.

"First of all,-quiet please-let me say this. Despite that latest word, I don't consider this an invasion. As you know or should know as being entomology students, the Sydney funnel web spider is endemic to this part of Australia. It's a part of this environment and of the ecosystem.

Unfortunately, from time to time, these creatures come in contact with humans. It's our responsibility as sentient, intelligent beings to do what we can to prevent them from entering our homes and to avoid all contact with them as much as possible. They don't hunt us. They just don't do that. Any confrontations with humans are purely for defensive reasons. It's very possible, in fact most likely, that these people who were unfortunate victims of this spider didn't utilize any ways of prevention to keep them from entering their living spaces. Their deaths are most likely also attributed to the fact that they didn't get the appropriate help in time for whatever reasons there may have been. They were rare, unfortunate casualties. Most people who get bitten by them survive after treatment with no lasting aftereffects."

Another hand went up. "Yes Susan," Mary replied to her.

"Professor, how do you explain the two spiders that were on that woman? Do they always kill in pairs like that?"

Mary wasn't sure what to make of that two-spider report. She'd have to see the report for herself. She knew who to contact for that.

"I'm not sure what to tell you about that. That is not what the funnel web normally does. In fact, I've never heard of that ever happening, even in this region known to have them. So as for explaining that, I can't. It could have been pure coincidence that there were two of them in her house. But I'll need to check that report out for myself before I can draw any opinions or conclusions about that.

"What I want to assure you is that there is no invasion. All it takes is one person to make up a story which may sound plausible, sound believable as he or she starts to convince others, and pretty soon you have a panic on your hands based on one fabrication. We, as humans, are susceptible to becoming victims of believable lies or made up stories if we let our common sense down and take things at face value. If you're going to be future scientists whether in entomology or some other science, you can't take things at face value. You have to be skeptical and search for the real truth. Now's the time to start doing that. If something doesn't sound quite right or sounds farfetched, you check it out and find the proof that it's true. If you can't prove it's true, then it probably isn't.

"Now arachnids were going to be our subject in a couple of weeks. I'm pushing that forward to next week because of what's currently going on and we will discuss in much more detail about this species and similar other ones. In the meantime, let's at least close this topic for now and start today's. If you'll turn to chapter 18, we'll begin."

That seemed to satisfy them, at least for the time being. The sounds of pages flipping assured her they were ready to move on.

10

December 9, Canberra, New South Wales

The autopsy had revealed heavy neurotoxin poisoning of her system. After all other possible causes had been quickly ruled out, the toxin had finally been identified as Robustoxin (d-Atracotoxin-Ar1) which was especially unique to the male Sydney Funnel Web spider. With the significantly larger amount of venom that had been injected into her, symptoms would have been felt by the victim very quickly. Death would have overtaken the victim quicker than the normal average time for such a bite. Tabitha Ingram likely suffered not only respiratory distress but also a dangerously rapid heart rate, uncontrollable muscular contractions and decreased or loss of ability to ambulate or even stand up. Her level of consciousness, or LOC, would have decreased to a level that would have required immediate hospitalization. In the end, she had multiple organ failure which led to cardiac arrest and death.

Had she been found in enough time before death overtook her, even though unconscious, she might have been saved with immediate appropriate first aid and transport to the nearest trauma hospital. Unfortunately, she wasn't discovered until hours later and by then it was too late.

Of course the media got a hold of what happened earlier on. Their reports of the death and somehow finding out about *two* killers instead of one only seemed to fuel the public's concern and near panic in some. Thus, the word spread like a rapid wildfire to and through the entire UOS campus in Canberra. It seemed like the word spread faster there than it would have on the internet, if one could believe such a possibility.

Starting that horrible day, just yesterday in fact, special precautions had been taken by all personnel entering the house, whether first responders, family, or friends. When Peter found out about what killed his wife, what he was told didn't alarm him to the extent that it should have. As he was getting ready to make arrangements for exterminators to thoroughly fumigate and spray the entire house from top to bottom with killer chemicals, he received a call on his cell from a number associated with the University of Sydney.

"Hello?"

"Good morning. Is this Mr. Peter Ingram?"

"If I am, who would I be telling this to?"

"I'm Mary Welling, a professor of entomology at the UOS. I heard about your wife and I am so sorry. My sincere condolences to you. I know this is a bad time but considering what happened I believe very much that you would be in serious danger if you went back into your house before it could be thoroughly gone over by professionals. I wanted to get in touch with you before you went in."

Peter couldn't believe this. Who was this lady?

"Dr. Welling, I appreciate your concern but who are you and why are you so concerned about this, about what happened to my wife? And why now? We're mourning you know. And, by the way, how did you get my cell phone number?"

"Mr. Ingram, I understand completely and I apologize again. To answer your last question first, I have a friend who works in the town clerk's office in Canberra. She helped me find out how to get in touch with you after I convinced her that it was an emergency regarding your wife. To answer your first two questions, I'm a professor of entomology, which includes study of arachnids-thefamily that includes spiders-and I considered this a matter of extreme urgency to the point it being a matter of life and death. I believe that your house may have an infestation of the spiders that killed your wife and if that's the case, you and anyone else in the house would be in serious danger; in fact, probably as much as your wife was."

Peter was shocked. Infested? What the hell...?

"Don't you think that's getting a little panicky? I mean, professor, if the house was infested, as you say it could be, don't you think that we would have noticed it before now? There are, or were, three of us living here. One of us should have noticed it by now. Besides, I plan to get it exterminated anyway."

"Well that's good that you're having that done. I recommend, and that's all I can do, that you not enter the building until after that's done. Mr. Ingram, how long have you been living there?" Mary decided to see if she could establish some kind of timeline from the time they moved in up until Tabitha's death.

"Oh, I guess about two years, give or take a month or two. Why?"

"Did you ever have a rat or mouse problem during those two years?"

"No, absolutely not. I would have gotten that taken care of in a flash if we had."

Mary was thinking if he had a rodent problem, the spider or spiders would have taken care of them if one or more was in the house.

"Ever leave any doors to the outside open or ajar, even screen doors?"

"Ah, I see what you're getting at. Well I never did. I doubt Tabby would have either. She hates flies and they tend to do what they do best-- fly right in when a door is opened. Course I'm not home all the time so I can only speak from what I've observed when I'm home. Anyway, is that all professor? I have to make some arrangements, including final preps for the funeral."

"Absolutely, Mr. Ingram. I'll let you go. I'd appreciate if you'd at least consider what I said and recommended. For the safety of yourself and your family. I apologize if I bothered you and I am truly sorry for your loss. You have my sincere condolences."

"Doctor, I'll consider what you said. One question I will throw back at you before I go. Can you tell me one thing: what kind of spider are you talking about here that you think killed my wife?"

Mary was surprised at this. Didn't anyone inform him?

"No one told you?"

"Hell, no. I was just told that a dangerous spider killed her but no one that I know or the person who told me saw it. Guess they didn't know either."

"I believe it was the Sydney Funnel Web. Not one you'd want to be anywhere near. Very dangerous to humans. That's why I was so concerned and *that's* why I wanted to warn you not to go back into that house until it's been thoroughly examined and treated appropriately by professionals and given an all-clear. If there's an infestation, no one should be in there without the proper attire and armament. Just one of those things is dangerous enough."

"How do you know that's the one?"

Mary anticipated he might ask that. "Because it's rare for any spider to kill a human unless the person is highly allergic, and the reported size as described by one eyewitness was similar to that of the funnel web. Was your wife allergic to bee or other venom?"

"Not that I know of."

"Well, they were too large to be regular house spiders from what was described. The fact that they were reported to be *on* your wife when she was on the floor and not having scurried for cover suggests their extreme aggressiveness, which is uniquely characteristic of the funnel web. Anyway, I'll let you go. If you have any questions, anything at all, please don't hesitate to contact me. My work number is on your caller ID I presume?"

"Yes, it is Doctor and thank you. I'll consider your advice and I do appreciate your calling me and your concern. I'll call you if I have any questions."

After giving her condolences one more time, Mary hung up, hoping he really would consider and then follow through with her advice. Although she couldn't be one hundred <u>per cent</u> sure it was the Atrax robustus, the spider was so dangerous that even being only fifty percent sure would be enough to advise taking extreme precautions-especially in this case.

11

December 9, Sydney, New South Wales

After she hung up the phone, Dr. Lou Ellen Binder sat there stunned for several moments. Her worst fears were realized which only deepened the mystery of Max's death. According to what she had read, Max shouldn't have died even from the Sydney Funnel Web spider. Cats didn't die from that. Was that information she read bogus? If so, and the rest of it was correct, why would *that* be incorrect? For now, she ended up with more questions than answers. She had the answer confirmed as to what killed him. The question remained why? She considered the possibility that the cat could have been allergic to the venom. Before she contacted Rodney, she had a phone call or two to make.

Contacting the New South Wales Department of Public Health, she had to endure several phone trees before she was connected to the correct division. That division, in turn, transferred her call to the New South Wales department of entomology. She hadn't been aware that the Australian state had its own entomology department. After the phone rang several times, it was finally picked up.

"Entomology, this is Manny Williamson. Can I help you?"

"Yes, I'm Dr. Lou Ellen Binder, a veterinarian here in Sydney. I'm calling because I've had a recent death of a feline patient who had died from a funnel web spider bite in the owner's home. I'm a bit perplexed about this because when I researched the effects of the bite, the website about the spider said certain mammals, such as cats and dogs, were not significantly affected by the bite. If that's the case, this cat shouldn't have died. I gave it a clean bill of health from my examination of it. I'm wondering how true that statement is that cats and dogs aren't affected by the bite from this spider."

"Ok. Uh, doctor did you say that the cat died from the Atrax robustus? The Sydney funnel web?"

"Yes sir, that's correct."

"Did you do the autopsy on it?"

"Necropsy. Yes, I did. Blood tests and toxicology tests confirmed the overwhelming presence of a neurotoxin associated with this spider in its blood and tissues."

"And you're saying this animal had no ongoing diseases or neurological maladies or any other afflictions of any kind?"

"That's what I mean by clean bill of health." *How clear can I make it when I say that?*

"Did this cat have any allergies? Could it have been allergic to the venom?"

"I'm considering that possibility. However, I want to see if there are any other possibilities before I come to that conclusion."

"Hold on a second doctor. I'm going to get one of our entomologists on the line with you. I'm a lab tech but I think you need to speak to him. Hold please."

"Ok, I'm holding."

After about a minute, a female voice came on. "Hello, Doctor Binder, this is Doctor Mary Clendenan."

"Hi, Doctor Clendenan. I assume your tech mentioned what this was about?"

"Briefly," Clendenan replied. "Tell me what you know, including what you found at your necropsy and blood tests, including toxicology."

Lou Ellen provided her with the information. "And do you know, or does the owner know, about how long the cat was dead?" asked Clendenan.

"No, I'm afraid not."

"I assume you are 100 per cent sure it was the Atrax robustus venom you found in its system?"

"Yes, there was no question. The toxicology lab I used confirmed it a second time after review."

Lou Ellen heard a soft sigh on the other end. She could imagine the entomologist thinking hard on this one, but realized she would probably not provide her with the answer that she wanted. This could be one of those situations where the buck stopped with her. It was *she* who was the veterinarian, not Doctor Clendenan. But, any information about this arachnid could help her with this investigation.

"Well, …may I call you Lou Ellen?"

"Sure. If I can call you Mary?"

Clendenan chuckled on the other hand. "Oh absolutely. Ok, Lou Ellen, here's what I can tell you. I can't explain why the cat died, unless it had been immunocompromised with some other affliction. Or, there's one other possibility."

"Oh? What's that?" asked Lou Ellen, now sitting straighter in her chair.

"Well, these spiders are, as you know, pretty nasty: in fact one of the nastiest and most aggressive arachnids in the world. Not only do they attack without much hesitation or provocation no matter how big the target, they can bite repeatedly and very quickly. The more they bite, of course, the more venom gets injected. Their fangs are among the largest in the arachnid family. And their toxin is among the deadliest among spiders."

"How do they compare with tarantulas?"

"Relatively speaking, tarantulas are not deadly or even harmful to humans unless one is allergic to its venom. And compared to the funnel web, they are only very mildly aggressive. One can even hold one without getting bitten. Not so with the funnel web. You don't want one in your house, let alone hold one. It would bite you before your hand even touched it. Tarantulas are not endemic in the Sydney area, so I doubt any are around, unless someone has one for a pet. Even if they were, as scary looking as they might be, they would not be a serious threat to a mammal or human, unless they were being obviously and intentionally threatened and physically abused.

"Now I'm not a vet, you are. But knowing about these things and their potent venom, I would consider the fact that if the cat was bitten repeatedly more than twice, then the combination of the venom potency and the amount of it injected would have been sufficient to overcome whatever initial resistance the cat's body might have had to it. Had it been any other spider, except for the Brazilian jumping spider, I would have seriously considered another explanation for its death. Seeing as your lab confirmed the cause of death, I would say the owner has a serious problem in his home. This means *he's* in just as much danger as his cat was."

Lou Ellen couldn't have agreed more. The problem wouldn't have gone away with the cat's death. She had to get a hold of Rodney Johnson as soon as possible.

"Mary, thank you so much for this information. I better get a hold of the owner."

"Any more questions, here's my direct number. And if you hear of any more incidents with others regarding the funnel web, get a hold of me right away." After giving Lou Ellen the number, they hung up.

Picking up the phone again, Lou Ellen looked up Rodney Johnson's number and dialed his home. No answer. She left a voice mail for him to call her as soon as he heard the message. It didn't matter if it was off hours or not. She was to have him get the answering service to call her. Then she looked up his cell phone and called that but he didn't answer that either. Again she left a message to call her asap, no matter what time of day or night. Then she made one more quick call.

With that, there was nothing more she could do for now. It was late, after 6:00 pm. The office had closed at five. Everyone else had gone. Shelly, the receptionist, had let her know earlier she was leaving. After Lou Ellen made sure all that should be locked up was, she made sure the few caged animals were fine, then turned out the lights, locked up, and was soon on the road to home. She was expecting Rodney to get a hold of her at some point that evening, which was why she had also told the answering service to page her immediately when he called. Every day was different in some way. Today had been one that was unique that she hoped would never be repeated.

12

December 10, Canberra, New South Wales

The funeral for Tabitha took place following the memorial service. The cloud covered skies seemed to make the day even more dismal. For Peter and Sandy Ingram and extended families on both sides, the loss was devastating. For friends and work colleagues, including Katherine Beasley, it was equally so. If one thought about the cause of her death, the tragedy of what should have never happened was unimaginably even more heartbreaking. Tabitha had been quite healthy. For something like this to happen, it could have happened to anyone anywhere. It was not something one could predict or anticipate and there were no red flags or warnings ahead of time. Who could have imagined?

The reception filled the small restaurant. Family, friends, and fellow workers of Tabitha gathered to dine together in fellowship as a final tribute in memory of her. It would take a while for father and daughter to get through the grieving process because of the sudden unexpectedness of her death. For them, it was a reality shock that was truly difficult to understand.

Conversations between different family members and Peter alternated between small talk and finding out information about each other among those who rarely saw each other or saw each other only at funerals. It was not the way everyone wanted it, of course, but it seemed that's the way it was and would probably always be that way.

As some of this conversation was going on, in the back of Peter's mind, there was the haunting thought of what had been reported and witnessed. Inside *their* home, on Tabitha's body her killers looking at their human discoverer defiantly, as if daring her to take their prey away from them. Although he had difficulty believing, or even imagining an infestation of such horrible creatures in their home, he had equal difficulty dismissing it as hogwash. In fact, despite his initial doubts, he found it nearly impossible to disregard the possibility of an infestation. He didn't want to talk about it to Sandy because he knew that would scare her. Especially in the restaurant here.

After Tabitha's death, he and Sandy had stayed at a motel until he could return the next day. He had planned on doing that, but something kept him from following up on his plan. It was not a feeling one could explain, but knew was there. So they stayed two more nights at the same motel.

Two days after the autopsy on Tabitha had been completed and the final report had been issued by the medical examiner, Peter was again reminded of the serious problem within his house by what the autopsy report had said. Sandy had known about the spiders and that had creeped her out to the max. He didn't want to believe they had a problem, that it was just two of those creatures. All the exterminators had to do was kill them and they'd be all set. Right?

He saw a small article in the ad section of the local newspaper about an extermination company that took care of all kinds of bugs and insects. He wrote down the name of the company, Bugs Away and phone number.

Today he had made an important decision. After he had thought about what Mary Welling told him, he realized he could not jeopardize his or his daughter's health or life by not taking care of what he now believed was a problem before they returned to the house. Something had to be done. However, before he arranged for special exterminators to blanket sweep the entire house from top to bottom to make it entirely spider and bug free and for them to stay at a relative's house for a couple of days until it was done, he had to return to the house to gather some important work items, medical and diabetic items, and more personal clothes as well as his medications to take with them. No matter the danger, he had to get those things, especially the medications and glucose monitor which he had to have. And then he had to retrieve the most important essentials of Sandy's in her room. He wasn't looking forward to the task.

Speaking with his brother Mike at the restaurant, he asked if he and Sandy could stay with them just for a couple of days while he had the exterminators do their thing. Mike readily agreed and added they could stay for as long as they felt was necessary, no problem. Mike's wife, Greta, agreed that they should until the problem was cleared at the house.

Peter was still upset and quite a bit stressed out from all that was happening, not to mention the death of his wife. After the reception, Peter got on the phone and called the exterminators to arrange for their arrival the next morning. He told them he had a serious spider problem but failed to tell them the type of spider. Whether it slipped his mind or he assumed they could take care of any types no one knew for sure. They advised him they would use chemicals and to make sure that he covered all exposed food, refrigerate or discard them, and covered everything he didn't want chemicals on. He was also advised to take all clothes and medications with him that he needed. The debugging and de-spidering, whatever they called it, would take an entire day and would involve destroying the creatures by chemicalizing everything in the house where they believed the spiders might come in contact with. The plan was to start as early in the morning as possible and continue working for as long as it took until they covered everywhere.

Once the agreement was made on the phone, they made an agreement to meet at his house in an hour and they would come by with the contract, collect a down-payment, and send someone through the house with full outfits that would be tough to be impermeable to the strong chemicals. They didn't really know what they would be dealing with but were confident they could handle it. They never had a problem on any jobs so far. One of the things their man would do was assess where the nesting areas were and the specific chemical they would use to destroy the creatures and their webs. His report would include the layout of the house and lay the groundwork for what they needed to do.

The risk would almost be like going into a tiger cage at a zoo in the dark. If you were uninformed, you might not know if the tiger was really there or not if you couldn't see it. You might sense it was there but couldn't be sure until it was too late. Even if you were armed, it might not be enough to save you if you were attacked.

In actuality and what they didn't know, was that they would probably have a better chance of survival or, at the very least, of not being attacked had they gone into a dark tiger cage than what they would soon be facing.

When they arrived at the house, Peter and Sandy looked at it. From the outside, it looked so peaceful and serene. So benign. On the inside, it would be forever different: empty because of Tabitha's permanent absence. But unfortunately, that was the least of their worries. Peter had to go inside there to find those things and get them out of there. He might run into a problem in there or he might not. He knew that running into that particular kind of "problem" could have serious consequences. There was no way he would allow Sandy to step even one foot inside there.

"Ok, honey, you know to stay here, right?" Sandy, even at the ripe old age of 11, never even thought of arguing that. She hated spiders.

"Daddy, you couldn't drag me in there right now. Are you going to get our stuff?"

"Yes, I am. Hey, want me to see if Amy's at home next door? Maybe you can play with her while I take care of things here."

"Yea, I'd like that. We gotta see if she's home first."

"C'mon, lets' go over there and see."

They got out of the car and went to their next door neighbor's house. Although they had gone to the funeral to pay their respects to Tabitha, they skipped the reception. After Rick Jenson answered the door and was pleasantly surprised to see Peter and Sandy, Peter first thanked him for coming to the funeral, then explained why they were there and their plans for the next couple of days.

"Why of course Sandy could stay for a while. Amy would like that. Come on in, hon."

Sandy came in with a smile. "Hi, Mr. Jenson. Thanks for letting me play with Amy." Then she turned to her father. "Daddy, be careful. And would you get Teddy and Petunia for me?"

"Sure, honey, I'll get them."

"Teddy and um, Petunia?" said Rick Jenson with a huge grin. He almost laughed.

Peter laughed. "Yes. Sandy named them. They're her two teddy bears."

"Oh, well, we better let Dad go. He's got an important mission to take care of," Rick said to Sandy. "Let's get Amy." Then he called out to her. Soon the girls were together and started doing what 11-year-old girls often do: play games.

Then Rick turned back to Peter, his smiling expression now turned serious.

"Don't worry, Pete. We'll watch her. Take your time and do what you gotta do. Be careful in there. You get in trouble, you call me. Here's my number." He wrote it down quickly on a scrap paper and handed it to him. "I heard all about it. Now I've got the heebie jeebies here, for cryin' out loud. I try to keep it covert, ya know what I mean, but my Amy has been noticing me lookin' around sneakily. I tell ya, it's hard to get anything by our young kids today."

Pete nodded. "You're right about that. We have to try and not scare them. Yet at the same time, we can't hide everything from them. In some cases should we? Ya know? In this case, we probably should at least make them aware of the possibility. Even though it's scary to even think about, gotta be prepared for it, whether you're a kid or not."

Rick nodded in agreement.

"Well, I better get over there and started getting the stuff together. The exterminators are also gonna be there shortly."

"When are they going to start?" asked Rick.

"Tomorrow morning, and it's going to be an all-day thing. We'll be at my brother Mike's house for the next couple of days. The exterminators will have my number and I think you have my cell, which I gave to you one time. Still have it?"

"Yea, I think I do. Somewhere. Why don't you give it to me again, just in case? Anything occurs about the house, I can at least contact you."

Peter jotted down his cell number and gave it to Rick. "Ok, buddy, appreciate it. Thanks. I'll be back when I'm done there to pick up Sandy."

While they were upstairs in Amy's room, Peter approached the house. He wasn't scared by any means but was more cautious than anything else. One thing he had decided before hand: he would not go down to the basement. Even if he needed something there, which he couldn't imagine what that would be, he wouldn't go. That was the area of his wife's death and not only was that where the killers were seen, it would remind him of what happened. He didn't need any reminders to add to his memories of the tragedy. So for him, that was off limits. He'd limit his movements inside to his bedroom and Sandy's. After he packed whatever he could that they would need for two days, he would be out of there.

He took the keys out and positioned them to unlock the front door of the raised ranch. Everything looked so pristine and neat on the outside. It was a very attractive house. He didn't think too much of how it'd look on the inside. But as he unlocked the door and started opening it, he felt the hairs on the back of his neck stand up and then those on his arms as the opening exposed a darker inside. This was not good.

13

December 10, Blacktown, New South Wales

The plant was really hot that day. Rodney's sweat seemed to be pouring out of him. Right now maintenance and air conditioner repairmen were working on getting the central air conditioners running again. This was the first time he could remember the air conditioners breaking down. It was actually very rare but it could and did happen. The goal was then to get them running again as quickly as possible so as not to cause any serious health issues among the employees.

Metal Dynamics Incorporated, was a relatively small company with only about 150 employees as compared to others in the region. It was located in Blacktown, a few miles west of Sydney. Known for its high quality products and excellent workmanship which other companies appreciated, it was a company that turned a hefty profit for the metal parts it made for engines and certain machines that other companies used to make other things. It was almost like saying, 'You make this good for me and I'll be able to make something good for somebody else' and so on down the line.

Rodney worked on one of the machines that he used daily. He considered it "his" machine, although he knew it really wasn't. It was just the only one he was assigned to and used and he enjoyed that. It was already about 2pm. The loud buzzer would sound, indicating their afternoon fifteen minute break.

Paul came over to him. He worked the next machine over in their section.

"Hey mate, let's get out there for a few. It's freakin' hot in here."

Rodney wiped the sweat off his brow. "Yea, sure is. Won't be much better out there."

"True. But at least we can get away from the machines for a bit. Man, I'm thirsty." Rodney reached over to the nearby table, and grabbed a bottle of water he had stowed in his insulated lunch bag. Soon the men were outside, discovering that there was a slight breeze which did make it slightly cooler than on the inside.

They liked this 2pm break because it meant there was only a little over an hour left in the shift, which ran from 7am to 3:30 pm. Before they knew it, the break was over, Rodney and Paul had finished their drinks and it was time to return to the grind.

Actually, it wasn't really a grind. Not for Rod. He enjoyed the work, despite the heat today. Most days it was cool because of the central conditioning the plant had. Metal Dynamics was a good employer which believed that if it could keep its employees happy, within reason of course, then production and quality would remain high. That philosophy had proved itself true. In addition to some of the other good benefits, profit-sharing was a regular benefit that all the employees enjoyed. It's *because* of the high profits that the company was making that it was able to provide them with that financial bonus.

Rod had been there for a good fifteen years, so his time as far as seniority was concerned, was pretty secure. Paul, his work colleague and friend for about five years, had been there for only about six years and was younger than Rod by at least ten years. But it didn't matter. They got along well and felt comfortable in their "guy" talk during their lunches and breaks.

It was almost 3:00 pm and Rodney had just finished smoothing out a part that was nearly ready for the final finishing touch when he felt a vibration in his pocket. Somebody was calling him on his cell. Now who could that be?

He stopped his machine, pulled out the cell and looked at the screen. Technically employees weren't supposed to use their phones on company work time; only during their breaks was it allowed. When he saw it was from the Sydney Veterinary Office, he thought it might be more news about Max. He obviously couldn't take the call here, and soon the vibration stopped. Not wanting to draw attention to phone use, he went to the men's room and checked for a voice mail.

"Hi, Rodney, this is Louise Binder. Can you call me as soon as you get a chance and before you step into your house if you're not already there? It's important. I'll explain when you call. You'll be able to get a hold of me, whatever time you call. Thank you."

He thought, "*Well that's strange. And before I step into the house?*" In the back of his mind, a thought occurred which he really didn't want to deal with. But it was there and he couldn't get rid of it. He wondered if that thought was somehow connected to what Binder wanted to tell him.

He returned the phone to his pocket and decided to finish his work and call her before he left for the day and after he punched out. He wasn't about to get in trouble over a phone call that could wait another half hour.

Concentrating on his work for the last 25 minutes helped him get through it much easier. If he thought about the call, he figured he might screw up on the last touches of the part. This was why he didn't like receiving calls during his work time. But he made it to the finish line, and soon the horn blast signaled the end of the work day for them. After lining up at the clock and punching out, he declined Paul's invitation for a beer at the local pub citing important phone calls he had to make, but promised to join him the next day there after work. Paul accepted that and soon they headed their separate ways.

In the car, Rodney called the number that was on his caller ID. The receptionist at the vet office answered and he explained he was returning Dr. Binder's call. She put him on hold for a few moments as he sat letting the car's a/c cool it down. Then he heard a loud click.

"Hello Rodney?"

"Yes, Doc, I'm returning your call from earlier. Sorry I couldn't get back to you sooner. I was at work."

"Oh, I'm sorry to have bothered you there, but I'm glad I caught you there rather than at home. You're not home now, are you?"

"No, ma'am. I'm still sitting in my car at work, Getting ready to head on home. What's going on?"

"I wanted to warn you that what happened to your cat could happen to you."

"What? What are you talking about? What do you mean it could happen to me? You think that spider could get after me?"

Lou Ellen sighed, planning in her mind how to explain and put it in the right perspective so he'd understand better. She didn't like the way she started out here. Quickly gathering her thoughts, she decided to bring him up to date on what he could be up against.

"Rod, what I'm saying is, your house could have one or more of those funnel webs still inside. They could be anywhere: in your shoes, your open drawers, under the bed, in your closet. Once they get into the house, they might tend to stay. A spider already got one of your cats. How do you know it won't get the other one? And then there's *you* we have to worry about. These things are not like black widows where you get sick for a while but then get over it and get better. This is what I found out from a regional entomologist.

"When the funnel web species bites, you don't get over it. Unless you're treated. In fact, without *immediate* treatment, you will die. And that's *without* being allergic to its venom. That's how dangerous it is. Not to mention the fact that it could bite repeatedly."

Rodney's jaw dropped. "You gotta be freakin' kidding me. Are you telling me that my house could be a death trap? This is crazy. I could just stomp on the damn thing. That'll squish him into bloody smithereens."

"Rod, I'm afraid it's not that simple. This thing is not going to let you do that."

"Not going to let me do that? C'mon doc. It's only a damn spider, not some human ogre that's waiting to pounce and smash."

Lou Ellen realized she had to penetrate through his denial and downplaying of the danger.

"Ok. Rod, let me explain. I'm going to give you an analogy that's right on the money with this 'only a damn spider'. Think of being out on the African savannah with its tall yellow grasses. Can you picture that in your mind?"

"Sure I can," he answered. "So?"

"Picture yourself as an antelope. Better yet, a *baby* antelope. You're grazing away from your momma. You look over the tall grasses and everything looks peaceful and serene. The sun is shining and it's a hot day as always. But because you're a baby antelope, you don't really care too much about those things. You just want to be near your momma and ready to feed. You don't know anything else right now. Are you with me so far?"

Rod nodded. "Yea, I'm with you still." He had a hunch what she was getting to, but she hadn't gotten there yet.

"By the time you see it coming, it's too late. The lion is already on you and has sunk its fangs and claws into you. You're done, and you're dinner. You never saw it in the grasses, but it saw you."

"And you think that's what this miserable creature does?"

'Basically, well, yea. It'll see you long before you see it. And just like the baby antelope, you won't see it coming until it's too late. It's the lion of the spider world, a top of the line predator and defender of itself and wherever it is. It's got countless amounts of hiding spaces, and..."

"Ok, ok, doc. I get the picture. What you're telling me is that this thing could attack me without warning from anywhere in the house and kill me."

Lou Ellen felt the tension nearly as much as Rod, even just explaining this to him. It wasn't just an unpleasant bit of information and news she was delivering. It was the means that could save his life. All she had to do was convince him of its truth.

On her end, she nodded as if Rodney could see her. "I'm afraid that's what I am telling you, and I'm sorry. But you need to know. And I strongly encourage you to get a special exterminator that deals with these kinds of creatures to have them go over your house very thoroughly before you return home."

Rodney rubbed his face in a movement of nervous tension and ran his hand over his sweaty head. "But all my things are there and my other cat Friskie. What am I supposed to do?"

Lou Ellen thought for a moment. "Well, all I can suggest to you is that if you need to get those things, maybe have someone go in there with you and sort of be a lookout while you gather your things. Not too many. It's only for a day or two the most. Get the cat and get out. Your lookout could make sure you won't be unpleasantly surprised."

"Yea, well he'd have to lookout for himself as well, ya know."

"That's true," she replied. "But that's all he'd be doing is looking out for the both of you. You have to focus on collecting things and gathering the cat and its food and litter box. You can't do all that and lookout as well without jeopardizing yourself. These things could come out of anywhere and anytime. They are very aggressive spiders, even without provocation. Even with a lookout, it'd be a risk for the both of you. But you'd probably stand a better chance coming out of there ok. Having one in there is bad enough. More than one and there's some serious trouble there, which is a true major understatement."

"Shit," Rodney muttered, knowing that he had to believe that, especially after what he saw happened to Max. Now he had to worry about Friskie.

"Ok," he said to her. "Guess I'll go. Have to find someone to go in there with me at least so I can get the cat, then maybe go over to my sister's place in Campbelltown. Know who's a good exterminator for this kind of thing?"

Lou Ellen said she did. After finding their number, she gave him the name of the company and their phone number. After thanking her and promising to honor her request and keep her posted with the results of his plans to take care of the situation, he realized he couldn't be in a hurry to get home. He was still sitting there while all the day shift workers had left. Now all the evening shifters were there. Could he find someone this late in the afternoon to go into the house with him? Who should he call first, a friend or his sister to request staying there overnight or for a couple of days? Or should he call the exterminator first? After some quick thinking, he decided on the latter and dialed their number.

14

December 10, University of Sydney, New South Wales

In the lab, Mary Welling looked at it in its glass enclosure. There was no way to sugarcoat its deadliness. As an arachnologist, she considered it beautiful, but that was purely subjective on her part regarding its description. It was a mother with lots of little spiderlings crawling all around it. She had to make sure not one of them would escape. It happened once before about a month ago when an enclosure was accidentally knocked over. There were two adults that had been in there, a male and female. There had also been babies. Although they had recaptured the two adults and as many of the spiderlings as they could, they suspected some of the little ones had gotten away because they were nowhere to be found. Counting them initially was virtually impossible, so that made it equally impossible to know for sure if all had been retaken or if some had gotten away. They had suspected the latter because it looked like there were less of them when they were put back in the enclosure. She had to make sure the same thing didn't happen again.

It moved slowly inside and turned. It was now facing her and looking at her as she neared her face to the glass partition. She knew it couldn't get her. Maybe *it* thought it could get her because it raised itself up in a defensive attack position showing its huge fangs. Even for an arachnologist, she had to admit it did look terrifying when it stood up like that. Knowing all about it, she preferred to continue studying it from a distance and not up close and personal. She may be a die-hard spider researcher and studier, but she was no fool. Just as with many other dangerous occupations, you had to know your limitations and stick with them in order to stay alive and well.

"Hey, what 'cha doing there?" the voice asked. "Looking over our friend again?" It was Tom.

"Ah ha!" she exclaimed as she sat up and turned to look at him. "Look who the wind just blew in. Yes, I'm looking her over again. It never ceases to amaze me how deadly such a thing can be."

"Yea, that's amazing alright. Since you have the female there, you don't have too much to worry about her. Have you heard back from that guy whose wife was killed? Um, Peter something, I believe."

"Oh, Peter Ingram. No. I talked to him about a week ago. Told him some things he should know including getting his house exterminated. I hope he followed through. Has my number in case."

She lifted the lid of the enclosure quickly and dropped a cockroach into it. The spider immediately pounced. Soon the insect was being liquefied by the spider for consumption. While the mother ate, its spiderlings continued to cling to the rounded black carapace in their continuous movements.

#

December 10, Canberra, New South Wales

The silence inside the house made it seem eerier. It was strange, this feeling he had of entering what was his home yet was more like alien territory he was exploring for the first time. Peter didn't like it at all. Knowing what was in there, or *could* still be in there, was not just scary but downright terrifying. If it had been a rabid dog inside, despite its life-threatening dangerousness, at least he'd be able to see it. This, this was something else. The threat was invisible yet present. For all he knew, he could very well be watched right now, from anywhere. There were countless dark spaces and enclosures they could be hiding in. He knew what they did to his wife; they could do the same to him if he wasn't careful.

The silence in the house was deafening. Only the clicking of the wall clock in the kitchen broke the silence, and the sounds of his footsteps. There were no sounds of clickings such as sometimes made by sound effectors for class B horror movies with creepy crawlies in them walking or running around.

He knew a "monster" would not come out from behind him and blitz attack him. This he kept reassuring himself with in order to keep moving forward as he was doing. Walking through the living room area, all appeared in order and in their proper places. There was nothing appearance-wise to indicate anything was wrong. When he entered the kitchen, he noticed only a couple of small plates in the sink that were ready to be washed and a number of washed dishes and utensils in the drainer that appeared to be dry. Otherwise, the kitchen was neat and clean. Tabitha always made sure she kept it that way, especially before going to work.

He looked to his right at the door in the corner where it led downstairs. That's the door he would probably never go through again. Even when the place was cleaned thoroughly by the exterminators, the horror of what had happened down there was enough of a psychological trauma to keep him from descending. The memories of her and being found down there were too much for him to bear. Thoughts of selling the house were starting to trickle into his thoughts.

The longer he stayed in this house, the more he felt the urge to sell and go somewhere for a fresh start. Hopefully they would be able to stay in the same school district as now so there would be no school transfer for Sandy. He'd have to take care of this problem first before taking up that issue.

As he made his way upstairs, he was unaware of the several presences that were watching him from within dark enclosures and under the sofa in the living room. They were still, hidden within the shadows. They could see and sense him. He was not within their reach. But should he come their way.....

#

December 10, Blacktown, New South Wales

Rod had connected with Gone-for-Good Pest Exterminators located a few miles north of Sydney. They had agreed to come to his house the next day to assess what needed to be done. He'd meet them there at 9:00 am. Meanwhile, he decided to contact his sister Celia to arrange an overnighter. After explaining to her what happened and what he needed to do, she readily agreed and welcomed him for as long as necessary until it was safe for him to return home.

"I just have to grab a few things, clean clothes and toiletries from the house and then I'm out of there."

"Rod, should you really go back in there? Don't you think it's far too risky? Maybe if you brought someone in with you?" she suggested.

He thought about what Doctor Binder said and decided it would take too long to find someone, especially at the last minute.

"No, no time for that, luv. Have to go now, get in and get out. Then I'll be over there. Might get there about five or six."

"Good. Just in time for a bit of supper. Good luck and see ya when ya get here."

After they hung up, Rod decided the time was now, and he finally left the parking lot for home. This is one time he didn't look forward to it

15

December 10, Canberra, New South Wales

As he climbed the stairs, his cell phone rang. It was Mike. He wondered what time he would be getting there for reasons regarding supper plans.

"I won't be long here. I just arrived a few minutes ago and I'm about to collect some stuff. But the exterminators should be here shortly. Once I'm done with them, I should already have all I need and I'll be on my way there. Probably be around 4 or so when I get there."

"Ok. Listen, mate, be careful, will ya? I know something about those things. Get outta there soon as ya can. Ellie will be biting her fingernails instead of food if ya don't get here by suppertime."

After reassuring his brother he'd be there, Peter returned the phone to his pocket and at the top of the stairs he headed down to his bedroom. The silence of the house with no one being there but some*thing* being there sent chills up and down his spine. He had to admit he didn't want to be there right now. He could feel himself becoming a little paranoid, flinching every time he first sighted a dark area or spot. *Nothing like feeling like a walking bag of nerves*, he thought to himself. Quickly he opened the closet door and just as quickly, after making sure nothing poisonous or monstrous jumped out at him, he grabbed the duffel bag he kept in there and started collecting only the fewest necessities he would need for a day or two.

Going to the bathroom, he grabbed his shaving needs and a couple of other toiletries, including his and Sandy's toothbrushes and the toothpaste and dropped them in the bag. After scanning to make sure he had everything from there that he needed and thinking in a hurry to ensure he had everything from his bedroom, he headed toward Sandy's bedroom to gather a few items from there. He didn't want to backtrack so whatever he might have forgotten would have to be left, unless it was an extreme necessity that couldn't wait.

Working as fast as he could, he looked around trying to figure in his mind what she would need for a couple of days. He scooped up some panties, socks, a small bra, and a couple of dresses. Once he had them in the bag, he checked around the room as thoroughly and as quickly as he could. Once he left, he didn't want to have to come back. Shoes, ah yes. He bent down to grab a pair of shoes and sneakers then stopped himself quickly. He checked the inside of them as best as he could. When he didn't see anything hiding, he picked them up and put them in the bag. Looking around one more time, he then decided that was it. Going down the hallway toward the stairs, the silence was broken by the sudden ringing of the doorbell. The exterminators were here.

"Just a minute, be right there!"

When he approached the top of the stairs, he stopped dead in his tracks. If he had had a bad heart, he very well might have had a serious heart attack at that moment. What met his view could surely have caused one.

From the stair top on down three steps, there was nothing but huge, black spiders. Only his mind screamed in silence, *where the hell did these freakin' things come from?* The normal human response to a life threatening situation kicked in within him. The fight or flight response was the only choices in the world he had at that particular moment. He had to somehow let the persons outside the front door know. So he yelled as loud as he could. "Help. Help me. Come in now. I'm in trouble!"

He wasn't sure if it was the exterminators or someone else, but for the moment it didn't matter. And, he didn't know if whoever it was heard him, so he yelled again, louder this time. As he heard the front door knob jiggle, he realized the damn door was locked. He forgot to unlock it from the inside.

At that moment, he noticed a couple of the spiders on the front line raise themselves up, displaying their huge fangs, then lower down and move forward toward him. He was no spider expert but it didn't take a rocket scientist to know that this was not just abnormal spider behavior: it was downright freakish to say the least. He couldn't understand it because he wasn't a threat to them. He had been trying to *avoid* them. Humans could never be their food. Yet, they seemed to be predating him. Why?

"Help! Come in. Break down the door if you have to!"

The line advanced forward, forcing him to back up toward Sandy's room again. He kept yelling and wasn't sure what to do. He thought about stepping on them, but there were so many that his chances of getting bitten were very high.

He decided to make a run for Sandy's room. Before he did that, he yelled down one more time, warning the persons now banging hard against the door to force it open that the floor was filled with deadly spiders. Although he recognized the species, his mind was such in a panic that he temporarily forgot the name.

Sandy's room was straight ahead and that's where he ran to, slamming the door shut behind him. As he looked at the window which had one of those false balconies that looked nice but couldn't be used as a balcony, he contemplated going out that and maybe jumping for it to escape the hoards of death creeping toward him on the other side of the door. He heard a loud bang coming from downstairs and realized it was finally forced open. Loud male voices assured him that rescuers, whoever they were, were here. He yelled down that he was in Sandy's room at the end of the hall upstairs.

"Holy mother of mackerel!" screamed one of the voices. "Mr. Ingram, it's Bugs Away Exterminators. Stay where you are up there. We're going to start dealing with this right now."

This was not what they expected to see. Unbeknownst to Peter, they had barely qualified with the regional licensing center and only a minimal rating was given to them for their relative inexperience in the type of work they would be hired to perform in order to get their licenses. It was almost like a roll of the dice before something disastrous happened *because of* their minimal qualifications. What they saw and had to deal with was beyond their limited capabilities. What they should have done was to dial emergency services on the phone, explain the problem and they would at least have gotten the fire department to get him out of the second floor with a ladder. Yet, they foolishly chose to take on the job themselves anyway. It would be a decision they'd later regret.

"Mac, get the two bifenthrin tanks. I don't think we'll have time to assess. Grab the special suits and gloves." Mac ran back to the truck to gather all that they'd need.

"Mr. Ingram, can you hear me?" the man yelled.

"Yes," he heard the distant reply.

"Are you ok, mate?"

"Yea, I'm fine, just scared enough to pee in my pants that's all."

"Ok, listen. My name is Ralph. I normally assess only but not today. You'll continue to be fine. Just give us a couple of minutes. If you're in the room with the door closed, you need to stuff the crack under the door with some kind of cloths or clothing. You don't want those bloody things to get in there. Do it now. In the meantime, we're getting ready to take care of them starting from down here. Whatever you do, *don't* open the door until we tell you to."

"Ok. I don't think you'll have to worry about that, Ralph. I'm Peter. I'm stuffing the door crack now."

"Ok Peter, good. You better find something to cover your nose and mouth temporarily. We're going to be using strong chemicals to get these things away from you. Chemicals might do the trick but first we gotta them away from where you are, so for now we'll use them. Be advised it's going to fill the house with very strong, powerful odors. We normally would never do this with anyone in the house, but under the circumstances, there's not much choice. So for your sake, please cover yourself. I'll let you know when to do that, just before we start spraying. You should open the window there if you can."

"Ok. I'll find something here."

Mac returned with the equipment and the two suits. What was supposed to be only an initial assessment for the job to be done was now a race against time to literally save a man's life. They could see that this hoard of spiders looked like the Sydney funnel web, but they couldn't be sure. The fact that they were all over the place told them nothing about the species. Infestations could involve any number of species. If they were being aggressive toward Peter Ingram, Ralph thought, that could be a strong indicator that this was the notorious Atrax robustus that was infesting this house. If that was the case, this man certainly was in serious trouble until they could eliminate the problem completely.

Like most Australians, they heard of them but never really ran into any of them on previous jobs. For whatever reason, they made the fatal assumption that they could kill them the same way as any other spiders.

Because the things were so nasty looking, they correctly suspected that even *they* would be in danger while they were in the process of exterminating. It was possible that what they were seeing, that stairway full of these things, might only be the tip of the iceberg. They had to be suited so well that not one inch of bare skin could be exposed. Their rubber extra thick gloves would be quite cumbersome to use but necessary to prevent the huge fangs of the Sydney to penetrate if attempted bites were made. Unfortunately, the thick, impenetrable material was in the wrong place on their body location.

Outside the front door, they donned their white suits, making sure they were completely covered, especially around their ankles. Their thick work shoes were the only other areas that remained virtually impenetrable. Going inside, they looked around for any more new appearances of the spiders but so far hadn't seen any others. They looked up the stairs and saw only one line of spiders. There'd been several when they first arrived. That meant they were advancing, likely toward where the homeowner was.

"Ok, Mr. Ingram, we're going to start spraying now. Cover up if you will, mate."

"Ok, I'm covered," he said with a now much muffled voice.

Their first priority was to first get rid of the spiders that were an immediate threat to Peter Ingram as well as themselves. One of them started spraying the toxic chemical on the stairs starting from the bottom and working himself up. At the top of the stairs, he continued to spray them and saw the numbers in the hallway were more than he realized initially. Even though he was suited and completely covered, he still had to be careful and not take anything for granted. Those fangs were like hypodermic syringes, razor sharp and full of poison.

When Mac joined him at the top, each worked side by side fanning the chemicals to cover all the spiders. They all started scampering away instead of collapsing. They had all disappeared into somewhere and parts unknown.

Then further ahead, what looked like the front lines of this spider "army" was shockingly at the covered crack to the door, behind which was Peter Ingram.

The two men looked at each other in shock. "Will ya look at this? These sons of bitches knew where the man was. How the hell could they possibly know that?" Ralph asked his partner, who could only shrug. He'd never seen anything like it before either.

"I tell ya," said Mac, "this is scary. I never seen any bug or spider do this. Not even rodents."

"Yea, me too." Ralph looked around them at the now dead spiders. There might have been at least fifty of them. "Reminds me of the movie "Arachnophobia". Now *that* was a scary movie. But, being Hollywood, you can figure that wouldn't really happen in real life, now would it, mate? Yet," he looked down around them, "look what we have here."

He sprayed directly on them. Some reared up, then dropped down and as the spray hit them, they all scampered away, the same as the previous ones. What the hell?

For a few moments, they looked around that spot to make sure none were still around and there weren't more that would suddenly pop out.

"Hey Ralph, how come they didn't fall down and die?" asked Mac.

Ralph shrugged. "I think like many other critters, it might take a little time for the chemicals to work into their bodies. They didn't like being sprayed on and ran away. In the meantime, the chemicals are working themselves in and they'll die where they ran to. C'mon. We better get Mr. Ingram out of here now before we run into any more surprises."

Ralph yelled through the door and Peter was finally able to step out.

"Oh thank God. Thank you fellas." Peter was breathing fairly heavily still holding the cloth to his face as the still-masked exterminators quickly led him downstairs and out the front door. After they were outside, the two men removed their masks to breathe in some fresh air. The air in the house stunk heavily of the powerful chemical they used and would need at least a full day to completely air out.

After collecting their thoughts, Peter thanked them again.

"Well, we were glad to be able to get to you. Those things," Ralph pointed toward them, "would most certainly have killed you and in no time flat. Just one could do the job, let alone fifty or sixty. But that, my friend, is bizarre and abnormal. They don't gather in hoards like that and don't infest like that. But these did. And what's got me is how they knew where you were hiding."

Peter looked at him in shock. "What? Wha--wha--what, they knew where I was hiding? How the *hell* could they know *that?* That's impossible!"

Ralph looked at him, equally as bewildered. "We found them lined up at the covered crack of your door, mate. Don't ask me how they knew. I'm just as confounded about it as you are. And we are professional exterminators. But they knew. Somehow. Might be a good idea to consult about this with some spider experts.

"In the meantime, let me get the contract, you can read it and sign, and we'll finish the rest of the house, top to bottom with the rooms we didn't do. We won't spray everywhere, just where's there's likely to be unseen creatures that we can't see for ourselves. I think the assessment now is a moot point."

"Ok," agreed Peter.

A few minutes later after he had read and signed the contract, he let them know where to contact him and went to get Sandy at Amy's house, while the two exterminators went back inside to continue the extermination process.

16

With bags of belongings in tow, Peter brought them to his car and then went to retrieve his daughter. Rick Jenson met him at the door and let him in.

"Hey, buddy, got what ya needed?"

Peter gave him a sheepish grin. "Much as I dared get, I guess. Place gives me the creeps knowing what's in there. And it's my own freakin place for crying out loud."

Rick looked concerned and understood the seriousness of his neighbor's situation, and especially after the death of his wife. Although he asked once before, he felt he had to ask again.

"Still doing alright there mate? Can I help you with anything?"

Peter nodded and tapped his friend's shoulder with a gentle fist. "Naw, Rick, thank ya though. All things considered, I could be doing worse. Besides, have to be strong for the little one, ya know?"

"Speaking of little one," said Rick, "let's go back there. Those two are having a good time." Peter followed Rick to Amy's bedroom where they were playing little girl games and having a ball. Peter thought it was good that she had a friend here. It was something to keep her mind off of the recent tragedy in their family.

Then the girls saw their fathers watching from the doorway. "Daddy, daddy, Amy asked if I could stay over tonight. Could I?" asked Sandy with that huge look of hope in her eyes.

"Yes, Mr. Ingram, can Sandy stay tonight?" little Amy repeated the question.

Peter smiled and looked at Rick. "I don't know girls. It's up to this fella here," he said nodding his head toward Rick.

Rick, of course, already had decided because he was asked earlier by Amy. "Sure. Why not. That ok with you, Peter?"

With that decided and said, Peter went back out to the car to retrieve a couple of items from Sandy's bag for an overnight stay. He returned with them and plopped them in a small bag in Amy's room.

"Ok. Listen, I'm going to go. Sandy, please behave yourself and listen to what Mr. or Mrs. Jenson asks you to do."

Sandy nodded with enthusiasm and joy on her face. "Ok, daddy. I'll behave. Don't worry."

After checking with Rick about a pickup time the next day and making it for 4:00 pm, Peter gave a hug and kiss to his daughter and left her with her friend to enjoy the rest of the day. He briefed Rick about the two men starting the extermination process next door, thanked him for having Sandy over and left to go to his brother's house. He would find out the results of the exterminators the next day.

#

While Peter had been in the Jenson house, the two men went to their truck for other equipment and chemicals. After deciding to use stronger ones, they foraged around the truck for a few minutes and took what they needed out of it. Checking themselves for the thick boots and rubber gloves they would still need, they considered themselves ready to go back in and were soon inside the front door.

"Let's start at the top and work down. If they're going to try to get away from us, better to go down than up," one of them said to the other.

"I hear ya. Ok, let's do it."

With tanks on their back and the ends of the hoses connected to the tanks in their hands, they made their way up to the second floor. Up there they started at one bedroom, sprayed everywhere they could where spiders might hide including the closets and under the bed and furniture, they continued going from room to room spraying every inch of the floor.

Making their way down the hall, they looked up to see what looked like a square trap door into an attic. They saw no handle and no apparent way to open it.

"Hmm," said one of them. "Looks like some kind of attic up there maybe. No way to get up there. Didn't see that before."

The other looked and said, "We can't go up there. Might as well just spray around it. Besides, there's no way those devils can squeeze through those tiny cracks. Let's keep moving forward, I say." The other man agreed and they continued their spraying.

As the two men slowly made their way from the top floor to the bottom, they looked carefully at, through, and under all dark or hard to get to areas as much as they could. In addition to looking for any more of the creatures, they were searching for webs as well. Most spiders, although not all, have webs somewhere, and as exterminators they would know, or should know, which few didn't. These that they had seen would have them and they were determined to find them. They feared that when they did, there very well might be more of them around.

Each man took a room and worked together on each floor. One wouldn't descend down to the main floor until the other was completed. They sprayed the chemical only where the spiders might lurk or hide.

"Ralph, I'm clear here. How you doing, mate?"

"Just finishing up in here," he replied from Peter's bedroom. Then he came out. "Ready to go down?"

They descended. So far neither of them found any webs. One floor done, two to go. According to Peter, they had a basement which consisted of storage areas and a laundry room. It was kept as clean as basements could be kept, from what Peter had told them. But they wanted to make sure the main floor was assessed and cleared of anything not wanted before they went down there.

As they started carefully searching the living room, Mac scratched a persistent itch on his right ankle. Although he tried as much as he could not to do that, the damn itch not only wouldn't go away, it seemed to torment him even more. After scratching it, he felt the huge relief and now he could continue his work.

Every room was carefully gone over with the kitchen being last. Once they sprayed around areas where creatures might come in, including all cracks and crevices, under the kitchen sink and dishwasher and window sills, they were finished here.

With his mask-muffled gruff voice, Ralph suggested they check their tanks to ensure they had enough to continue downstairs. If either one needed replacing, they had plenty of them in the truck.

"I think I better replace this one," said Mac. "Feels pretty light."

"Yea, me too. Do me a favor and replace both of them."

With a nod, Mac took both tanks and in a couple of minutes returned with full ones. Now they were ready to go down.

On Mac's right ankle, a thinner area of material became exposed between the tight pants cuff and the top of the work boot, although that was not something he could be aware of unless he looked at it. In most situations, that would not be an issue and could be ignored.

They looked at the door leading down to the basement. It was not something they chose to rush through. Based on some, although not all, previous experiences as well as their notoriety for spooky or bad things to occur within them, basements were considered harbors for all kinds of creepy crawlies such as silverfish, cockroaches and other bugs and, of course, spiders of all kinds. The largest majority of the latter were harmless. They just *looked* scary but actually posed no real threat to people. Try telling *that* to an arachnophobe, Ralph once told a friend when asked what kinds of things he ran into in his work.

"You ready mate?" Mac asked.

"Yea, let's go."

Ralph opened the door. It was dark down there with some light coming through an unseen window. He looked for a light switch and found one on the wall to his left. Switching it on brightened up the stairway and the first room at the bottom. Because they hadn't done an initial assessment of the entire house before starting their work, they were walking into unfamiliar territory. It was not something they liked to do because it gave them no opportunity for any kind of strategic planning which was often necessary for what they had to do.

At the bottom of the wooden stairs, they saw to their left what looked like a storage room. Just inside that room, they noticed a door on the wall which, they presumed led to the outside. The stairs led into a fairly clean-looking room with the washer and dryer to their right. Beyond that, to their right in another room is what looked like the furnace sticking out from just beyond the door threshold.

"Looks like we have three rooms down here," observed Mac.

"Yea. Appears that way. Listen, I'm going to spray the crack at the door up there and then come back down. Why don't you start over there in that storage area? If we're going to find any webs, this is where they might be."

Mac nodded and headed toward the storage room, while Ralph went up the stairs and sprayed the door crack. If any spiders they encountered tried to go up there, they would be stopped dead in their tracks. Literally. As he descended back down, he sprayed the stairs as well. They didn't want to take any chances. Not with these critters.

At the bottom, he let Mac know he'd be doing the furnace area.

Mac walked carefully through the relatively small room. It had several boxes in there. There were two small basement-type windows near the top of the walls, indicating they were below the ground level. He didn't notice any webs so far but he sprayed all around the windows anyway. All cracks he saw were sprayed along the wall corners and, of course all along the floor where it met the walls. He sprayed all around the boxes, trying not to saturate them and get any of the chemical on them. He noticed they were sealed shut, which he was glad about. Spiders and other things liked to crawl into dark places, and open boxes would provide the perfect opportunity for that. These would not provide that. One less thing to worry about, he thought.

Back in the furnace room, Ralph was doing the same thing. Even though they didn't have a lot of experience under their belts, they remained as consistent as they could in their tactics and in the organized way they performed their tasks. No matter what the job was, if they left one bug behind, then they didn't do their job. A good standard to start out with. So far he too hadn't found any webs. *That's really strange,* he thought to himself.

"Hey Mac, did you find any webs over there?"

"Nope. Nothing so far. I take it you haven't either?"

"Naw, nothing. I don't understand it. Where the hell did they come from? Haven't seen any more of them either."

They continued to spray. When Ralph finished in the furnace room, he started in the laundry area around the machines. He looked behind and under them, but saw nothing and no movement of any kind. He sprayed there anyway and around the small window which let in the daylight from above the ground. There were a few small webs around it, he noticed but no spiders or other bugs. In fact, it suddenly hit him that he noticed not one bug, silverfish, ant, cockroach, whatever anywhere in any part of the basement.

Usually, basements always have *some* bugs down there. It's just the way it is being below ground. They crawl from the outside through the smallest cracks. He knew that's what bugs did. Yet here, there was not one sign of life.

"I'm getting ready to open the door here," Mac told him.

"What, the door leading to the outside?"

"Yea."

"Wait til I get there. You never know what you'll find behind closed doors. Hang in there for a minute, pal."

Ralph checked under the wooden stairs and sprayed thoroughly under there as well, even though there was nothing there. Coming back around, he entered the storage area. Both stood near the closed door.

"I gotta admit, this is a first for me. Nothing here. Not one blasted web. How the hell can that be?"

"And no critters of any kind," replied Mac. "That's pretty odd, don't you think? For a basement?"

"Not even a fly. I saw a couple of small regular webs back there," he said, pointing back toward the machines, "but there was nothing. No spiders around and they would have been pretty small to make those. Probably just regular house spiders. Not a sign of it or them around. That's pretty unusual, I'd say."

Then for some reason, Ralph felt the blood drain out of his face when he looked at the closed door. He didn't know why. A feeling of dread suddenly washed over him and he felt a little bit of a cold sweat break out. It was like sensing an unseen presence. A dangerous one. You didn't see, smell, or feel it, yet you knew it was there.

The last time this happened, he was suddenly and unexpectedly faced with the deadly brown snake that had somehow gotten into the house. He was aware that it was one of the most venomous snakes on the planet and was known to have killed a lot of people who didn't get immediate treatment. That was a couple of years ago. He hadn't been faced with anything that scary or felt that way. Until now.

"Hey Ralph, what gives, pal?" asked Mac, suddenly concerned. "You look like you just saw the infamous headless horseman coming at cha."

Ralph looked at him with a deadly seriousness that Mac hadn't seen for quite a while.

"Mac, ole buddy, listen to me. We're not going to open that door here."

His partner looked surprised. "Not open it? Why, what cha thinking?"

Ralph looked down in thought and then back up again at his partner.

"We need to first see how this exits to the outside. We gotta see if there's the typical outside basement door that you lift up to open and there's stairs going down to the regular lower door. That's the way I'd like to do it if we can, rather than open up this one. It would provide us with plenty of light once opened up and a means of easy quick escape. We can attack, if necessary, from above and it would be much safer, in case there's anything between this door and the above ground one."

"Sounds like a good plan. Except for one thing: most people keep the above ground cellar doors locked. And they lock by a latch which is on the *inside*."

"Ah, shit, you're right. I forgot about that." Ralph looked at the closed door.

"Alright. Son of a bitch. Guess we'll have to tackle it from here. But, I want to first make sure that outside door *is* locked. I really don't want to open this door unless we have to. Be right back. And don't open the door until I get back."

Five minutes later Ralph was back. He shook his head, indicating to Mac that they would have to open this inside door.

"You ready?"

Both checked their tanks. "Ready," said Mac.

On the count of three, Ralph pulled on the knob but the door wouldn't open. "What the hell?" exclaimed Mac. He pulled again but the door wouldn't budge. "Son of a bitch," muttered Ralph. Then he saw the problem. "Oh for crying out loud!" he said loudly, and turned the lock mechanism to the open position in the middle of the knob. When he pulled again, it opened. Cool air came rushing out of the light-free darkness. So did something else.

17

December 10, Sydney, New South Wales

Rod knew that he was going to do what he shouldn't be doing. Going in there with someone, at this point, was definitely not an option. After parking in his driveway, he went to the garage to get the cat carrier. He'd need that to transport Friskie to where he was going. He needed to get her and his things out of there and as quickly as possible. Doctor Binder had warned him to be on the lookout for anything in the house that shouldn't be there that was related to what had happened. In other words, unusual looking webs.

He stepped inside and got to work right away. First things first, he thought. Have to get Friskie. "Here girl. Friskie, here girl. Come on to papa."

He looked around. Only the clicking of the wall clock in the kitchen broke the silence in the house. He didn't see her. Sometimes she clambered under the sofa or bed to get cozy and cat nap. He knew that's what cats often did, and his was no different.

Putting the cat carrier down, he called out to her again as he walked around. She didn't appear out of any of the rooms. In the kitchen, he noticed the wet cat food in the dish was only partly eaten. Most of it was still there from this morning. In the bathroom, he looked to see if she was in the litter box. She wasn't there and there was no litter that she might have left. In the back of his mind thoughts began to flash which now started entering the front of his mind. That brought the memory of Max to him. Now, he was starting to fear the worst. *Oh my God. No, not Friskie.*

He looked everywhere but couldn't find her. It was very unlike her to not respond when he called out to her because she was always happy when he got home. She always would walk or run up to him and rub herself against the bottom of his legs to let him know she was glad he was home again. Not this time. Could it be that somehow she knew that something had killed Max?

He was glad now he had only one floor. There was no basement, but rather just a crawl space in which he never went down into and never wanted to store anything down there. It was too dirty. Besides, he had his garage he stored stuff in anyway.

In his bedroom, he checked everywhere, including under the bed and behind it. Opening the closet door, he checked inside. He ignored the small hole in the lower right corner of it. It had been there since he bought the house a few years ago and because it wasn't interfering with anything or allowing anything in, such as mice, he didn't bother with it. Besides, he considered it a little too small for a mouse. While he had it open, he took out a small suitcase he kept in there and took down a shirt and pants, and then threw a couple pairs of clean underwear and socks in there. That's about all he needed from in this room. He would gather his toiletries after he found Friskie.

For some reason, he happened to look up. *There she was!* On top of the high book case in the corner of his bedroom. It was next to his computer desk.

"There you are, girl. Oh man, what are you doing up there? C'mon down, girl. We have places to go, people to see. C'mon now!"

The cat didn't move, which was odd. She was alive alright and looking down directly at him. But her behavior was a little off kilter. She always responded to him before. Sometimes it took several calls but she would always give in and come to him when he called. Again, not this time. Something was up and this was a good indication that all here was not as it seemed. He felt instant goosebumps on his arms and a chill run up and down his spine.

He then realized that something was keeping her from coming down off that bookcase. If that was the case, it could not be good. Looking around, nothing seemed out of the ordinary and nothing was where it shouldn't be. Everything was in its place. So why was he feeling his blood running cold?

The cat knew something and definitely sensed something. "Shit, you ole girl, why couldn't you talk to me and tell me what you know, eh?" he asked the cat, knowing full well he spoke out loud for his own benefit. The cat kept looking at him, then at something over his shoulder. He noticed her eyes shift and looked behind him to see if he could see what she was seeing. There was nothing there. He looked back at her. She seemed to be looking in the direction of his closet but he couldn't be sure. The closet doors were closed. He looked back at her and she was still staring at them. *What the hell?*

Turning around, he walked slowly toward them. He couldn't imagine what he would see, if anything. He'd just been in there and there was nothing there but his clothes hanging. No monsters or other things to jump out and get him. Yet the cat stayed right up there looking at the closet. Something here.....

Sliding the right side closet door to its left, he looked around inside and then looked down. There was the hole he had ignored and failed to look at down in the lower corner at the back wall near the floor. It was pitch black and led to what seemed like an empty space. Then he realized, for the first time, that it might lead to the crawl space below the house. Why hadn't I thought of that before, he thought to himself.

But there was something whitish that seemed to be filling the hole. It appeared translucent, filled the hole opening and, when he looked a little closer, appeared to widen then narrow further in. He couldn't see beyond that. Then, he thought he saw something dark blot out the whitish whatever it was he was looking at. Its subtle movement startled him. "Holy shit!" He backed off suddenly and slammed the closet door shut. He didn't know for sure what he was looking at, but he sure as hell didn't want to stay to find out. Picking up the phone in his room, for lack of knowing who else to call, he contacted Doctor Lou Ellen Binder and asked to speak to her immediately. This was not something he could wait on. If he couldn't get her on the phone, he'd try and grab the cat and get out, clothes or no clothes.

Sensing the extreme urgency in Rodney's voice, the receptionist paged Lou Ellen to pick up the phone for an emergency call.

"Doctor Binder here. Rodney, what's going on? Are you alright?"

When Rodney explained where he was, what he was doing, and briefly what he had just seen, he thought he heard the doctor softly gasp over the phone.

"Rodney, describe exactly what you saw in that closet, or thought you saw."

Describing it as much as he could and then telling her about the dark something he saw blot out the whitishness, he heard nothing but silence on the other end for a few moments. What he didn't know was that she was quickly thinking about and remembering what she had found out in her research and with talking to certain people. She now was convinced she knew what he had seen, even as briefly as it was. She kept her voice as quiet and calm as she could. The last thing she wanted was to panic him.

"Rodney, listen to me. Get out of that house now. Did you find your other cat, what's her name…?"

"Friskie."

"Yes, Friskie. Did you find her?"

"Yes I did."

"Then get her and get out. Grab whatever couple of items you need and leave as quickly as possible."

"I'm having trouble getting my cat down from the bookcase. She won't come down. What am I supposed to do?"

"Rod, listen to me. Your life is in danger. What you saw, that whitish thing, was a funnel web. You saw it inside a hole in your closet floor?"

"Yea, right where the wall joins the floor."

"Do you have a basement in your house?"

"No, just a crawlspace."

"Damn", she muttered softly. "Alright. Where are you now in the house?"

"In the bedroom."

"I strongly suggest you go to another room with the phone."

"But my cat…!"

"Rod, listen. Right now the cat is the least of your worries. Let me know when you're in the other room and I'll explain."

Reluctantly he left the room and went to the bathroom.

"Ok, I'm in another room. The cat is still up high on the bookcase."

She wasn't sure where that was, but that seemed to tell her the cat was ok for now.

"Ok. Your cat should be ok for now. This is what I believe you saw in your closet. The whitish thing in the hole is a funnel web. That is in sync with a funnel web spider. Based on the fact that Max was killed by a Sydney funnel web spider, it's more than likely that's what you saw. You know, believe me that you don't want to be in the house with one of *those* things."

"Doctor, you're damn right I don't."

"What I'm concerned about is the funnel web in a hole that likely leads to a crawlspace below your house. They're probably using the web as a conduit to get through the hole from down below which is likely nice and moist for them. They like that from what I found out. It's possible they are living in your crawlspace. And, if you find one, you might find another. Get my drift?"

"Doctor, I can't leave without my cat. She's too precious to me and she's all I have left."

"Well, Rod, I can't tell you what to do. All I can tell you is if you don't leave soon, you may not leave at all. Do you have family?"

"Yes, three kids from a divorce."

"Think of them, then. If you can't save your cat, then at least save yourself. But please leave now. If there's more than one, which there probably is, and they come out, which they might, then you'll have even less time to get out than now. Promise me you'll leave now."

"Ok."

"I'm going to hang up now. When you get to your destination, would you do me a favor and call me to let me know you're ok?"

After promising the doctor, he hung up and went to get the cat carrier. He would try to coax Friskie down as best as he could. Going back into his bedroom, he saw the cat still up there.

He called for her, then looked over at the closet. "Oh my God!" he said out loud. The closet door on the right was partly open, exposing the darkness inside.

He hadn't thought of it before but when he slammed it shut, it bounced back open part way from hitting the side. Now he knew time was definitely not on his side.

Going close to the bookcase, he reached up and did his best to get the cat to jump into his arms. "C'mon girl. C'mon down, you'll be ok." His increasing panic mode seemed to extinguish his presence of mind, because he failed to think of closing that closet door.

#

Inside the closet, the black creature slowly emerged from the web, followed by an unknown number of its brethren. The large leading male looked ahead with its multiple eyes. Although it could move quickly, it chose not to. It was not necessary. Time was definitely on *its* side and somehow it seemed to know it. But it needed to keep moving in order to let the others out as well. It noticed the light coming through and was attracted to it and therefore pressed forward.

18

December 10, Canberra, New South Wales

Ralph Nesbit had been in the business of extermination for at least 20 years. In fact, his father had gotten him into the business after he had graduated from high school because his father had owned an extermination company. Fresh out of high school and not sure what he was going to do for the rest of his life, he was actually thrilled when his father made him a job offer right away in the family business. Without contemplating very much about his future, he knew that he would like working in the extermination business. He didn't know why, he just did. Once he started, he stayed with it, even after his father had passed on, leaving him the business.

As had been expected at the time, he had enjoyed playing the role of bug buster, although he had several times admitted that it had its challenges. Some of the cases he had taken on involved hoarding cases of such extremes that the sight alone would be enough to make anyone vomit, let alone the smell of food putrefaction, cockroaches, and mouse or rat droppings among the huge trash piles. Of course neither he nor any other extermination company would take on jobs where there was hoarding unless the trash piles were cleared out. This is what he'd been doing mostly, although there were "clean jobs" he had also, where there were just bugs and other vermin but no hoarder's piles of trash and junk. He was kept so busy with these jobs that the thought never occurred to him that he could make even more money if he became certified in extermination of the more dangerous invasive creatures of the insect, arachnid, and reptile worlds.

This certification would require investing money for mandatory training and then being tested by the regional government for the certification process. If one passed the test, then the special license would be issued to that person.

Mac Devlin was the follower who'd been working only for about seven years in the business. Compared to Ralph, he was a rookie, although he was knowledgeable and competent enough to do the job. When Ralph had needed to hire an assistant, he took on the young Mac who was eager to learn the extermination process. If Ralph was willing to train him, he was willing to learn. But it was quite a learning experience, because he had to know not just about the different kinds of vermin they would have to deal with but also about the different kinds of equipment and chemicals they had to know and which ones to use for which kinds of vermin. It wasn't just a just-go-in-and-spray kind of job. It was much more than that. Even with all the previous training, without the *special* training and certification required for confronting and eliminating properly certain kinds of dangerous creatures and despite their combined years of experience, they were not ready for this: for what they were about to encounter.

It was a foolish decision that Ralph made and one that he'd regret for the rest of his life. No one knew what made him decide to tackle with this enemy. Later, in retrospect even he didn't know why he moved forward with his decision. Almost immediately he saw what they were in for. Both gowned and masked men stood gaping in horror, with their chemical tanks and hoses facing forward.

Nothing could have prepared them for this. It was almost like opening the doorway to death. Two large funnel webs clung to the cement side walls and stairs. There were, what appeared to be, dozens of the deadly spiders facing them. One moved quickly as they both sprayed everywhere inside that space. They covered the walls and stairs with the deadly chemical, which caused most of the webs to quickly collapse, but not the spiders.

Unfortunately for them, as well as the owner, what they *should* have known they didn't. This was the moment Ralph realized he made a huge mistake. He could see for himself that the chemicals were not having the effect that he had expected. He knew that the creatures' failure to collapse from the chemical meant that this wasn't working on them. What he *didn't* know was that this was not the appropriate treatment for this kind of problem. That's because he never obtained the proper training for this.

"Mac, don't make any sudden moves," he told his assistant. "The spray isn't having much effect on them, but it'll keep them from getting to us temporarily."

They were like an army facing the two men. Every so often the front line advanced forward toward the men and then stopped. The men kept spraying in their attempts to keep them at bay. Although the spray was covering them, for some reason it didn't cause them to collapse. As long as they kept inching forward, it wasn't killing them either.

"Ralph, what's happening here? This stuff kills everything. Why isn't it killing these sons of bitches? It's just like upstairs!"

"I don't know. Maybe their skins are too thick. I never saw anything like this."

Suddenly several of them darted forward very quickly. The two men were backing up while they continued to spray. Despite the chemical's apparent ineffectiveness, it was all they had.

"Mac, I think we better get the hell out of here."

As they backed slowly toward the storage room entrance, a line of spiders darted forward with some running off to the side. Ralph realized these creatures that were thought to have no brains or any form of intelligence were trying to surround them. He may be no highly qualified exterminator let alone an expert in spider or insect intelligence, but he knew that this was certainly abnormal behavior to the max.

"Let's go, Mac. Run."

Just as Mac started to turn toward the doorway, he felt a burning sharp pain in his right ankle, then another one on his left. "Ahh! Oh shit, ahhh!!" He lifted up his right foot while the spider continued to sink its huge fangs into him. Then another one crawled up his suit on the left side, followed by another. Another bite on his left thigh and another one below his right knee. He yelled like he'd never done before, which frightened Ralph as he turned and started to run back toward his partner.

As the huge amounts of toxic venom quickly coursed through his system, he started getting extreme muscle twitching and his vision became doubled. The pain was indescribable and he became numb around his mouth which made it extremely difficult to understand what he was trying to say.

Ralph realized his partner was in serious trouble and if he didn't get him out of there now, he could quickly die. Despite the fact that he was placing himself in as much danger as Mac, he couldn't just leave him there. Grabbing him as he started to go down, he managed to get Mac back through the doorway of the storage area into the laundry room. He saw several of the funnel web spiders on Mac and with his thickly gloved hands, whacked them off of him as quickly as he could. He didn't have time to look to see if the spider army was coming for them.

As he held on tightly to the man, he started pulling him up the stairs. Mac made feeble attempts to help with his feet and legs, but the extreme pain, muscle twitching and weakness made it nearly impossible. He didn't realize it at the moment but Mac was beginning to exhibit respiratory distress.

As he continued to pull upwards, Mac seemed to become heavier. "C'mon, Mac. C'mon buddy. You can do it. You can make it. Help me help you, mate."

Ralph inched upward ever closer to the door and near the top of the stairs. Looking down he saw a few of the spiders emerge through the doorway into the laundry room. "Oh shit. Oh no, you damn little devils. You ain't getting to us."

He pulled Mac up another step. Mac was now nearly dead weight and not saying anything.

"Hey buddy, you still with me, eh mate? You still with me?"

Ralph didn't have time to see if he was still with him. He kept pulling upward but it was becoming more difficult. His progress was very slow because of the now-dead weight of his partner. His quick glance down told him several spiders were now at the bottom of the stairs. Had they chosen to, they could have easily caught up to him.

With his adrenaline pumping and his heart thumping rapidly in his chest to get the needed blood pumped throughout his exerting body, he hauled Mac up another step until he was just below the door. Almost there, he thought.

With his left hand, Ralph grabbed the hose while holding onto Mac with his right. He sent a stream of chemical spray back down to the spiders which seemed relentless and determined to get him. The spray covered them and the steps but it didn't stop them. Their exoskeletons prevented the chemicals from being absorbed into their bodies, so they were well protected.

Several spiders were now on the bottom step. One had climbed up on the step above that. They were indeed coming for the two men. Ralph had the fleeting thought of revenge by them for the men breaking up their webs. Just the outrageousness of that thought made him quickly forget it and haul Mac up to the closed door itself. Holding onto Mac with one arm, he turned the doorknob and opened the door into the kitchen. Realizing the spiders were coming up the stairs seemed to make his adrenaline kick in more because he pulled harder than ever and got Mac halfway through. With the rest of whatever strength he had left, he got the unconscious man all the way in and quickly closed the door.

Before he checked Mac, Ralph had the fortunate presence of mind to look for and find whatever materials he could use nearby to block off the crack under the door to keep them from coming through. Once that was done, he pulled Mac out of the kitchen into the living room of the house. Then he checked him and what he discovered was not good.

His eyes remained open. His pupils had enlarged. Ralph was not medically trained except for CPR, but he knew that his partner might be dead. The open fixed eyes gave him his first clue. He checked for breaths but there appeared to be none. His lips and face appeared bluish. He looked for rising and falling of the chest but didn't notice any movements. Picking up his cell phone, he dialed the operator to get emergency medical services to the house promptly.

With the emergency person on the line, he was advised that if he knew CPR, to attempt it on his friend. He was certified in it so he made the attempt. Every so often he felt for a pulse but with no luck.

About five minutes later, EMTs and paramedics showed up and quickly took over. Vital signs they took showed no heartbeat, or respirations. They checked his pupils which were now fixed and dilated. Cutting off the top of the suit as quickly as they could, they applied the defibrillator paddles directly to the now bare skin of his chest and abdomen, with the wires leading to their portable machine and with it made three attempts to restart his heart.

Another paramedic not directly involved in the resuscitation procedure called the ER and spoke with the attending ER physician. When he asked and was told the patient had been unconscious for a few minutes, but it was uncertain whether it was six or more minutes or less than six minutes and then was told the patient had likely sustained serious multiple spider bites, the ER doctor advised that if they couldn't bring him back now, to call it. He asked that if a spider specimen could be obtained, they could at least ID the culprit. The paramedic looked at Ralph.

Ralph looked at the paramedic dead in the eye.

"I tell you this right now, mate. Anyone who tries to get a specimen of this killer is virtually committing suicide. You won't find *me* going back down there," he emphasized with the downward movement of his head. "And I strongly advise you not to go anywhere *near* that cellar door. That's where we came through. The entire cellar is full of these killers. Full of them! I'm calling the regional health department right now. Then I have to call the owner of this house. I better do it before it really hits me that my colleague and friend might be dead!"

The paramedics did their best to revive the man. Now and then they'd get a faint heartbeat and they did what they could to keep him going. They had neither antivenom with them nor the knowledge of what kind of venom that brought down this man. Then Mac's heart stopped once again, but this time they couldn't get it restarted. After about six minutes with defibrillations and heart stimulant injections with no response from the patient, they called it, and informed the hospital.

Going outside into the front yard, he made his two calls, while the EMTs gathered up the body and put it on the stretcher. One of them called the coroner because it would now have to be transferred to the morgue rather than the hospital.

The hardest part was yet to come for Ralph: notifying Mac's family. The reality of the sudden unexpected tragedy had yet to sink in.

19

December 10, Sydney, New South Wales

It was pretty difficult to keep a clear head and stay as calm as possible considering the situation he was in as well as his proximity to danger. If he was panicky, his cat would sense it and possibly cringe away, making it even more difficult to get him off of there, if not impossible.

As Rodney kept calling his cat, he seemed to be making some progress because it inched closer to him, alternating her looking between him and the closet door. He quickly glanced over his shoulder and softly under his breath said, "Oh shit." He again looked at the dark opening. Its threat seemed to be larger than the room. Now he sensed his time was becoming shorter and more limited. If he didn't get Friskie down within the next couple of minutes, he might not make it out of there. So far nothing emerged from the opening. Even though he knew it was only a closet, still it harbored potential death within its black interior.

He felt the adrenaline rush inside of him at the same time as fear gripped him. He kept looking back at the opening then back at the cat desperately trying to reach the fear-stricken cat with its eyes wide open in terror. She didn't seem to understand that her owner was trying to save her and get her out of there.

He stood on his toes to give him a little more height and felt the warm fur-bodied cat. Slowly, ever so slowly, he was able to get both his hands on the cat's body and positioned his fingers to grip it and bring her down.

Suddenly he felt her body go rigid and some of the fur stood up as she started meowing.

"C'mon girl. We gotta get outta here. C'mon sweet thing." Then he had her in his grip and held her loose enough not to hurt her but firm enough for him to maintain his hold on her until he could get her in the carrier.

Quickly glancing over his shoulder one final time, his eyes widened as he saw several black legs ever so slowly emerge from the black opening, then more appeared. They were coming out.

With a gentle pull, he got the cat off the bookcase and quickly ran out of the room, heading directly for the cat carrier and putting Friskie in it. There was no way he was going to stick around and gather any of his clothes. He may not be the smartest cookie in the package but he wasn't stupid either. Clothes can easily be replaced. Lives can't be.

Within minutes, he was gone and en route to his sister's house. With his cat safe and sound, and himself as well, he hoped this would be the one and only nightmare he ever had-especially one that had become reality. All kinds of thoughts raced through his mind as he drove the twenty-five miles to Campbelltown, which was southwest of Sydney. He'd never felt such terror before, especially when he saw numerous black spider legs start to emerge out of that darkness. Seeing things like that could give anyone nightmares.

On the way, he decided to stop at a small clothing store and buy himself a clean outfit to wear for tomorrow. At another store, he picked up a few inexpensive toiletries just to get him by for a couple of days. Before he left, he contacted the exterminators again. He had to tell them about that hole he'd found in his closet. They needed to know that.

He made the call but got only voice mail. *Damn! They must have closed up shop for the day.* He decided to leave the voicemail anyway. They might hear it first thing in the morning before they went to his house.

"Yes, this is Rodney Johnson out of Sydney. I have a couple of your chaps coming to my place in the morning to exterminate a funnel web spider problem I have. I need to tell you, and I hope you hear this before you send your guys over that there is a hole in my bedroom closet, right side on the back near the floor. I saw some of them big spiders emerge from there. And once they are done, if they can somehow cover up the hole so nothing else can get through there, I'd certainly appreciate it. Thank you. You have my phone number." Then he hung up.

With a sigh of some relief knowing he did all he could for today, he started backing out and was looking forward to seeing his sister again anyway. That might distract him, at least a little bit, from the stress of what happened and what the plans were for the next couple of days.

#

December 10, University of Sydney, New South Wales

After Mary and Tom had heard the news about the exterminator's death and its cause, they debated with each other regarding these A. robustus sudden occurrences all over the place, the several deaths that were retold in brief by the news media and the latest one; and their relation to the accidental spillover and possible loss of a large number of robustus spiderlings that had simply vanished into the unseen cracks and crevices of the lab that fateful morning two months ago.

What seemed to be happening were not the normal occasional confrontations between humans and Sydney funnel web spiders. This seemed to be an outbreak, with large numbers of them appearing in homes and actually becoming a serious threat to the community. So far, from what they have determined from reports, three people had died, and a couple more had been bitten but survived because they received the appropriate treatment on time.

They also heard a rumor that a cat had died but they hadn't seen any reports to substantiate that. Mary decided she wanted to check up on that on the off-chance that it was true. If it was, she would like to know why that cat died when it shouldn't have.

#

December 10, between Sydney and Blacktown, New South Wales

At his brother Mike's house, Peter was physically settled in temporarily, although the same couldn't be said for his feelings. Two days after the funeral, Peter was on bereavement leave from work and Sandy bereavement absence from school. As with anyone else, their loss would be felt for many years to come, perhaps for the rest of their lives. The cause of her death was not as easy to accept as a natural death because it had been anything but natural. It would be etched in their minds forever.

Mike and his wife Betty had welcomed them in for several reasons. They were Christians and would welcome anyone into their home. Because Peter and Sandy were family, their welcome was time-wise, unbounded by deadlines and limitations. Their grief over Tabitha's death nearly equaled Peter and Sandy's because she was family too, in relations and spirit. Mutually comforting and reassuring each other and Mike's reassurance that Tabitha had to be in heaven and was much happier now than she could ever be here on earth did provide comfort to his brother and niece. They were grateful to hear that.

While Mike was at work and would be home sometime within the next half hour or hour, Betty was in the kitchen making the typical kitchen noises one makes when either washing and drying dishes or preparing a meal. Peter was in the living room watching TV, then looked down and was reminded of the paper laying there on the coffee table.

Picking it up, he started scanning through it, then went back to the first page. He started reading one main story which was about a bank robbery gone bad in Sydney after an inept robber opened a bag of money after waiting too long and dye burst all over his face when he looked in the bag. It seemed comical when he read it which caused a chuckle to come out of him. The story concluded on page three and that's where he went. He wanted to find out if police nabbed that clown. After he finished, he scanned the page quickly with intent to continue his reading on page one when something caught his eye and for him it was a true mindblower.

The article wasn't a large one but was significant in size to catch anyone's eye. The headline did more than catch his eye. It read, "Death of Exterminator Attributed to Funnel Web Spider." As he read it, his worst fears had just worsened.

"Betty can I use your phone?" he asked.

"Oh sure you can, Peter. You don't have to ask. Our home is your home while you're here."

"Thanks, luv." He picked up the wireless phone and dialed the Bugs Away pest control company. Voicemail only. *Damn! Doesn't anyone ever answer the phone anymore?* He left a message for someone to call him either at this number or to his cell phone.

Now he felt even worse because another death was caused by something in his house. This was becoming worse than a nightmare. He felt bad for the guy who died. But why did he die? The article didn't say, except that what they had used to try and kill the creatures didn't work. The fact that there was an "army" of them, which was unheard of in itself was unbelievable. The two men were simply outnumbered, overwhelmed by sheer numbers, and were virtually defenseless against the onslaught of creatures that certainly didn't behave normally like any other spider of their kind. He was glad that Ralph survived. The article had said he was being treated at Sydney Hospital and would be observed overnight at the very least to ensure his full recovery from the one bite he had suffered. Pete wondered how he was able to survive and the other guy wasn't able to. Maybe he'd pay a visit to him in the hospital. It was obvious that he and Sandy could not return to the house anytime soon. At least not within the next couple of days. He'd have to find another exterminator. But to visit Ralph, he'd have to move fast. The guy might be discharged tomorrow and he had no clue where he lived. He really needed to talk to him.

Before he drove off, he always turned his cell phone on. He had kept it off to conserve the battery. His plug-in charger had unfortunately been left at the house in their haste to leave. After it was on, it pinged several times. That was the ping of a voice mail that had been left. When he checked it, he discovered it was from someone at Bugs Away.

"Hi, Mr. Ingram, this is Susan from Bugs Away pest control. I need to advise you to please not return to your house. Under no circumstances should you return. The problem still exists, except it's far worse than

expected. I'll explain when you return this call. I can't explain details on a voicemail. Please call as soon as you can. We are open from 8am until 4:30pm. Thank you."

This made him want to talk to Ralph even more.

"Hey Betty, I'm going to take a run to Sydney Hospital to see someone. I'll be back but if I'm not in time for supper, please don't wait for me."

"Oh, ok, Peter. I'll keep it warm for you if you're not back in time."

Fifteen minutes later, he was just a few miles away with various thoughts running through his mind. It was only when he arrived at the hospital that he found himself focusing on why he came here. One of the things he needed to find out was why the exterminators couldn't handle the fight against what they were supposed to be experts at. With one of them dead and the other in the hospital, something was very wrong. Professional exterminators, to his knowledge anyway, had never gone out on a job and ended up being killed by the very creatures they were paid to exterminate. That made no sense at all. He left his car and went inside to see if he could solve this perplexing mystery.

20

Sydney Hospital was a large, ten story hospital with an extended wing on each side of it. Those wings extended from both out the front and the back of the main building. It had a trauma center with a level that would be equivalent to a level III in the US, and was considered one of the finest hospitals in Australia. It was also a teaching hospital, affiliated with the University of Sydney and had a full range of physician staff, ranging from third and fourth year medical students all the way up to full attending in nearly all the medical specialties. If Ralph Nesbit was to get the best care for his treatment and recovery, he was in the right place.

After Peter hung up, he started leaving the parking lot when a call came in on his cell. *Damn, that was fast,* he thought believing it was Gone for Good Pest Control, the company he had hired. After being assured that they took care of spiders, including the infamous Sydney funnel web and was state certified in that, he knew he made the right choice. Unfortunately, this call was not from them.

"Hello?"

"Hi, yes, is this Mr. Peter Ingram?"

"Depends on who's calling."

"Hi, Mr. Ingram, this is Dr. Mary Welling," she replied with the assumption she was talking to the right person. "I'm in the entomology department associated with the University of Sydney. I specialize in Arachnida, particularly the Atrax robustus."

Peter's eyebrows lowered with a confusing frown. "The a--trax robust--what?"

Mary sheepishly grinned, having incorrectly assumed again that the person she was talking to knew all about it like she did. *I really have to stop doing that,* she chastised herself silently.

"Oh, I'm sorry. Bad habit on my part. It's the scientific name for the Sydney funnel web spider. Anyway, I'm researching into the apparent outbreak of these things in people's homes. I'm only calling certain people with out of the ordinary experiences. I had talked with a veterinarian in the Sydney area regarding any reports of attacks by them on animals in general to see if she had had any. I had thought that a cat killed by another animal was yours. Turned out it was someone else's. But it still shocked me. I still wanted to check with you. She mentioned two reports she had heard about, one of them was concerning the deaths in your house by what was believed to be caused by these spiders. I just had a couple of questions. However, if you don't want to talk, I'll respect that and won't bother you again."

Peter rubbed his neck, as he was thinking. He wanted to get going and didn't want to talk while driving. He did that once before and almost ran a stop sign for doing that.

"And you specialize in this species of spider?"

"Yes, I do. I also admit that I'm a bit taken aback by the unusual aggressiveness of them in your house. I know they are one of the most aggressive species of spiders and fearless of nearly everything. But their behavior in your case seemed far beyond the norm for their kind. Usually their aggressiveness is triggered by defense against a perceived threat to them."

The scientist's information indicated to him that she was who she said she was and that she certainly seemed to know what she was talking about.

"Ok, I have just a couple of minutes, and then I have to run."

"Thank you, sir. I'll make it quick. Question one: had you seen any spiders around your place around the time or before the tragedy?" Mary made sure she didn't come out and accidentally say "before discovering your wife's body." That would have been a fatal tactless error on her part.

"Uh, no I can't recall seeing any."

"Did you ever have a bug problem on a regular basis that you normally took care of and then the bug problem stopped suddenly at some point not long before the tragedy?"

"No. Wait a minute." He thought for a few moments. He did remember there seemed to be a decrease in the average number of bugs he normally saw in a given time period before Tabitha died. He hadn't done any home anti-bugging during that time. In fact, it had been about a week before she died that he had done some home spraying. His place was far from being overrun, because he would take care of any bugs he found as soon as he could. He was a true blue bug hater. Somehow he got caught up in other things and didn't spray around that week like he normally did.

"I did notice a decrease in bugs during the week before my wife's death. I hadn't done any spraying."

"I see," Mary said, now thinking the reason why.

"I had no clue we had this problem. Hadn't seen any of them in the house itself. I rarely went down to the basement because I kept all my tools and work stuff in the shed in our backyard and a few in the garage.

The only one who went downstairs to the basement on a regular basis was my wife. Not once did she ever tell me there was a spider problem down there. So you can imagine the shock I felt that terrible day. Worse day of my life. I wanted to die myself seeing her gone once I found out she really was gone.

"I can assure you that had these been regular house spiders, I would have packed up and moved out of the country. If regular house spiders looked like these, I wouldn't want to be anywhere near here, that's for sure. I hate those buggers."

Mary decided she'd heard enough to formulate her thoughts and conclusions about what may be happening in the Sydney area. Despite the fact that she had a sinking feeling about where all these spiders came from, she had to move forward and try to come up with any ideas about how to eliminate this outbreak. After thanking him for his help, she hung up and sat there for a few minutes to think this thing through. She didn't know what she could do, if anything. But if anyone contacted her for advice or information, she'd be as ready as she could be.

In the meantime, Rodney Johnson pulled out from his house and headed over to Campbelltown. He had talked with the exterminators from Gone for Good and let them know he'd be at his house before 9am and wait for them to show up. He'd tell them about the hole then and where they might be infiltrating the house from. In addition to that, he wanted to know what they would do and use to kill the spiders. He had about a 45 minute drive so he had plenty of time to think about things, and plenty of things to think about.

Sydney Hospital, New South Wales

After he had hung up with Mary Welling, he continued on his way from the parking lot. Even though it was now late afternoon, almost evening, Peter had to find out. After he checked in to the visitor's desk, he was directed to the fourth floor, Wing E, Room 422, bed 2. There he would find Ralph Nesbit.

Upon his arrival, Ralph recognized Peter right away. He was surprised to see him but was glad to have a visitor. Underneath his happy welcoming demeanor was the grieving, troubled soul of a man who had lost someone; in this case, his partner and friend. His normal, cheerfulness was kept subdued by the unfortunate circumstances.

"So how are you feeling?" asked Peter. "You are damn lucky, mate. I am so sorry about your colleague. Even though I hardly knew him, still it was a tragedy that should have never happened, ya know? What could ya do?"

"Hey, Mr. Ingram. Nice to see you, despite the circumstances. What a surprise. I feel kind of crappy but it could have been a lot worse. They have anti-venom pumping into me right now with this IV."

Peter looked at the hanging bottle and the tube leading down to his arm.

"This is what saved me. And the fact that I only got one bite."

"Well, thank God for that. And the anti-venom, which I didn't know they had. I'm sincerely glad you made it. Really. And you can call me Peter. It's ok."

Ralph looked demurely at Peter, fully realizing now the fatal decision they had--*he* had-- made before the confrontation. That decision cost his colleague his life, and his almost as well. He knew that if he told Peter the truth, it could not only mean his license and job, but his entire career as well. Yet at the same time, how could that compare to a man's life? You can get a new job and start fresh, but you can't bring a man back to life and have him start fresh.

"Ralph, what happened? If you survived, why didn't he? It was bad, wasn't it?"

The man looked at him, the tears welling in his eyes. He nodded, barely getting out a "yea". It was the reply of a man who'd obviously been so traumatized by what he'd seen and experienced and then trying to save his colleague's life but failing in the end that he was likely to be troubled by it for the rest of his life. It's possible he'd end up with PTSD.

"It was pretty bad." He hesitated for a few moments, as if trying to regain his bearings and control of his emotions. Peter could see it was somewhat difficult for him, but the man was trying. "I wouldn't a wished it on my worst enemy." He took a deep breath, prepared for what he was about to say. This is not something he could keep to himself with good conscience. He was responsible for what had happened and now he felt he needed to pay the piper.

"Have to tell ya something, Pete. I'm to blame for what happened."

Peter looked at him in sudden astonishment. "What? No, how can you think that? Those things were there when you got there. That was not your fault. The fact that they attacked both of you. No, I don't believe for one minute you were to blame for that. You certainly didn't cause your partner's death."

Ralph looked at him, knowing his next statement would be the revealing one.

"Well, sir, in a sense I did. I'll tell ya how."

Ralph told him about the multiple bites Mac had received all over him right through the suit he was wearing. The combination of the multiple bites, likely repeatedly by each spider, and the lack of immediate treatment had sealed the poor man's fate, while he had received only one.

As Peter listened, he was again surprised to find out what he hadn't known from the very beginning. It seemed to become even more tragic to him as he realized that had he, Peter Ingram, done his homework, this man might be alive today. In effect, both he and Ralph were at fault. Ralph, for choosing to take on the job they weren't officially qualified for, and *he* for not checking to make sure they were certified and qualified to tackle the job of Atrax extermination. Now he knew why this all happened.

After Ralph finished his confession and Peter stated his conclusion that both of them were at fault, Peter claiming more fault than Ralph because Ralph ended up in the hospital, they remained silent for a couple of minutes.

Finally Ralph spoke up. "Peter, although I can't help you anymore, this tragedy has really opened my eyes. I may not return to the job, I don't know. But, I want to tell you that you need to find qualified pest killers. Ones that are not only officially certified but well experienced in killing these things; this particular species. I don't know what kills them, but it's not the usual chemicals that kill others. We made that mistake. Don't find someone that does the same thing. That would be your mistake."

"I can't imagine what kills them if chemicals don't," replied Peter.

"Something does. And we didn't have that something. Find someone who does, find out what it is, and I recommend getting a second opinion. Once you get that second opinion, then you can pick which of the two you'll go with. But they both should have the same funnel web killer method or methods. If both are totally different, then get a third. But you need to move quickly on this. Those things, I believe, could totally infest your house. And then, my friend, your only option could be to just burn the house down. That's the last thing you want."

Peter looked down and realized that he didn't want this tragedy leading to another. He would take Ralph's advice and do this first thing in the morning. He wasn't sure about the burning down the house part, but knowing these things and the huge threat they were, that idea, however terrible, didn't seem implausible.

"Can I ask you one more thing Ralph before I go? Can't stay long. Have to get back for supper."

"Sure, fire away. I'm not going anywhere."

"First, knowing you hadn't tackled these things before, why did you choose to do this? Especially since they seemed to overwhelm you in numbers."

Ralph looked at the wall in front of him, in anger mostly at himself.

"Pride, Peter. Pride and anger. That's what drove me forward to try and destroy these things. I wanted them dead real bad and I thought we could do it with what we had. Those two things got in the way of the truth. The truth would have set us free and better, qualified people would have been called in right away. I made a very bad decision, and now I've got to live with that for the rest of my life." He then broke out in tears again.

What could Peter say? He felt a tremendous amount of sorrow for the man. As a man and also a sensitive person, he felt bad to see another man cry, or any person for that matter. He couldn't leave without giving him some kind of reassurance, something he could hold on to.

"You have family, Ralph?"

"I have a brother and sister. Both live in the Northern Territory."

"Wow, that's quite a ways away. Want me to contact them for you?"

He shook his head. "No, thank you mate. I called my sister. Told her I'd be ok and would be home probably tomorrow. Would be too far for them to travel just for one day."

"Not married?"

"No. Divorced. My wife-my ex, that is, left me for another man. I guess she didn't like being married to a bug killer." He tried to say that lightly, but Peter could sense an underlying sadness to that statement.

"I'm sorry to hear that. Really am." Now Peter was almost in tears. This man had a terrible burden to carry for the rest of his life. But his belief that life needed to go on perpetuated him to get Ralph to know and believe the same thing.

"Listen, here's my number." Peter wrote it down on a slip of paper. "Call me anytime if you want to talk. I mean that. And maybe we can keep in touch and get together sometime when you're feeling up to it. Might be in a different place by then. But my number will be the same. Now," he pulled out another slip of paper. "What's yours, my friend?"

Ralph gave it to him. It seemed to lift his spirits up a tad, but any amount would be a good sign.

"Ya know, I really appreciate you coming by here and then saying what you said to me. Most people would have liked to sue the hell out of me and seen me ruined for life. You did just the opposite." He was in tears now. "And I thank you very much for that. And I'm real sorry about your wife too."

"Well, pal, we both have things to be sorry for. But, we have to move forward. Took me quite a while because of a death, and will probably take you some time also. But you eventually have to get back on track. We all do. I did. So now, in order for me to let you start to get back on track, I'll let you get some rest. Thanks for the info. Listen, I will be in touch. And you should, too. How long you think you'll be here?"

Ralph looked at the board across from his board, not reading it but estimating in his mind when he might leave.

"According to the nurse, I have one more bottle of the anti-venom they have to drain into me, then another 24 hours for observation to make sure I don't suddenly develop a bad reaction. So far so good with the three bottles I've had. One more to go. I'd say, probably another couple of days and I should be ready."

Peter nodded. "Ok. Good. Sometime after you get home, give me a jingle. Maybe we can go have a beer somewhere to celebrate your hospital emancipation and recovery."

Ralph gave a smile, halfhearted, but a smile. "Sounds like a plan. Thanks, Peter. Thanks for coming by. I'll keep your number. I promise I'll get in touch. Believe me, I'll be ready for that beer." They shook hands with their new found friendship established.

At the door, Peter gave Ralph a thumbs up. "Until then..." he said. Ralph returned the thumbs up with a smile.

Five minutes later, he was in the car on the drive back to Mike's house. He found out what he needed to know, and established a new friendship at the same time. How awesome was that, he thought to himself? He felt sorry for Ralph because he had no one in his life. Although he made a bad decision which was a fatal one, he knew that everyone makes bad decisions in their lives. No one is immune to that. The fact that his contributed to the death of his colleague would haunt him for the rest of his life. Perhaps this was a time when he really needed a friend. Peter was glad he was able to become one to him. Besides, he had few friends himself so he knew it would be mutually beneficial.

He also knew that Ralph survived because he was very lucky; he had received only one bite; whereas his colleague Mac had received a significant number of them. When you realized that only one bite could be fatal without immediate treatment, he couldn't get over the fact that the poor guy had received enough bites to probably kill all the people in a small town. It was scary to think about that. No wonder the man died within minutes of the first bite. He had stood no chance whatsoever of coming out of there alive.

Before he knew it, he had arrived back at the house.

21

At 6:54pm, Rodney received a call on his cell phone. His caller ID said Gone for Good. '*Finally*,' he said to himself.

"Hello."

"Hi. Is this Rodney Johnson?"

"Yes, it is."

"Good evening, sir. This is Doug Wilson from Gone for Good. Sorry it took so long to return your call. We've been kind of swamped with calls the past couple of days. Usually when we get a call and answer with Gone for Good, some people wonder whether we're asking or telling them."

That got a laugh out of Rodney. "Really? You don't say?" he said, laughing again.

It was followed by a laugh on the other end. "Caller ID is sure convenient. Yet we still get people to just say hello when they answer and we have to tell them we're Gone for Good. We get that a lot. We were thinking of changing our name because some people start to wonder if we're really here, know what I mean? It's funny, but heh…

"Anyway, we got your message. We were out on a job. As for your case and what you requested, no problem. We appreciate you letting us know about that. That will help us focus on where the nesting area is."

"Well I'm glad you got the message. I would have been there in the morning before you guys anyway cause I would have needed to let you know about that before you went in."

"Good that you were going to do that. Extermination of these spiders requires a nonconventional nonchemical method, and knowing where the nesting area is crucial for this operation. Without that information, it would be extremely difficult for us to do this, or for any other specialized exterminator."

"Ok, Doug. Have a question for you. You mentioned chemicals don't work on these spiders. Why not? If they work on other spiders, why not these?"

"Well, from what I know about them and it's not a lot, the males wander all the time, go in and out of homes. The chemicals get on the ground and because the males' abdomens seldom touch the ground, they have little chance of getting the chemicals on them to kill them. In addition, they have a hard carapace, or exoskeleton is what the experts call them. That could keep the chemicals from being absorbed into their bodies. Much of the time, from what I've been told, in the past the chemicals just aggravated them. In other words, made them "mad" if such a term can apply to them."

"I see. So then what do you do?"

"Once we know where the nesting area is, we take water. Lots of water, like from a hose and it would be continuously running until it's turned off. We find the webs and destroy them and all the spiders we can find with the water."

"Are you serious? *Water* can kill them?"

"Yes. If we get them in their nesting areas, which are usually under things or in holes. The water prevents them from escaping and they will drown. That's why I mentioned the importance of you telling me about that hole. This is the best, most effective way to exterminate them. However, it does not guarantee that more won't appear in the future. This extermination gets rid of only the current problem and is not preventative. When this job is done, we can give you a printout of the best ways to prevent any more from coming into your house."

Rodney was amazed that something as simple as water was used. Somehow there always seemed to be another surprise right around the corner.

"So we will be there at 9:00 am. I strongly recommend you not come in while we're there. When we believe we've destroyed them all, we will inspect your crawlspace downstairs because you indicated to us that's where the hole leads to."

"Oh man, you're going down there?"

"Only after we're confident we got at least most of them. Going to the actual source of the nesting area is a rare thing because most web holes are inaccessible. This one happens to be accessible so we're going to take advantage of it. Don't worry, we will be wearing proven, impenetrable suits, gloves, and gear, even to their big fangs. Even nails have a tough time penetrating what we'll be wearing."

"What happens if you still see some down there?"

"We'll have our trusty hose with us, and will blast them to kingdom come. We're prepared for the wet as well. It will be messy for sure, with mud or anything else. But we've had messy jobs plenty of times, and this won't be the last either."

"Ok, then, Bob. I'll see you at 9. This oughta be interesting, I should say."

"We'll take care of the contract and payment business in the morning before we start. We'll assess the entire house first. In fact, the job might not start until the following day, depending on how long the assessment takes. I assume at this point, much of tomorrow will be assessing the what, where, and how we'll do the job. We'll want to thoroughly see where you found the problem and make sure for ourselves that's where the main source of them is coming from, as well as the *only* source. We hope that's the case, but if there's more than one location where they are emerging from, we'll need to know that before we even bring in the equipment. This might be a big job. Probably won't actually begin until day after tomorrow. Are you prepared to stay away for a couple of days?"

"Yes. I'll be staying at my sister's."

"Good. Well then, we'll see you in the morning. Have a good one."

"Thanks, Doug. You too."

After he hung up, he sat there on the sofa for a few moments thinking about what was going to happen at his house, while he digested the meal that Celia had served him an hour ago.

"So what's going on there?" asked Celia, with sisterly curiosity and concern.

Rodney told her all about what they were going to do. Then Tony, Rod's brother-in-law came out from the bathroom, having heard the conversation.

"That's unbelievable," he said. "Chemical poisons don't kill the blasted things, but water does. All I can say is, I hope we don't get those things in this house. That would really freak me out."

"Yea," Celia said. "Tony's got arachnophobia. When *he* freaks out, he's scarier than the spiders."

Rodney laughed. "Well, I better make sure I'm not around when you do, Tony."

"Well, I'll tell you one thing. It'll be in a pig's eye that we get any of them in this house. I'll blast them all to kingdom come."

"Yea," Celia said again, looking at Rodney jokingly. "He keeps a five inch cannon stored in the garage just in case, fully loaded." Rodney laughed again.

"Hey, luv, you're just a barrel of laughs today, aren't ya?" Tony didn't take it personally cause they often teased each other. It was all in fun and never taken seriously.

"Well, the exterminators are going to give me a printout of prevention methods, I won't have to worry about them returning, provided I stick to it faithfully. I can ask for a copy for you if ya like?"

Tony and Celia agreed. While they sat in the living room with the two men sipping their bottled beer and watching some TV, Rodney decided he hadn't spoken with the kids for a while. He decided to call them and excused himself to go to his bedroom and make the call before they went to bed. At ages 11, 9, and 6, the two girls and boy were still hitting the sack fairly early because they had to get up early for school. Because of his amicable relations with his ex, there was no problem for him to talk with them at least once a week. This would be that once. Five minutes later he was talking to one of them. It was always the highlight of his entire day when he talked with them. Even for just a few minutes. Every other weekend he could have them visit him, per the court and his ex's permission. Thank God for friendly divorces, he told himself.

22

December 11, Blacktown area, New South Wales

Peter was on the phone that morning to call another exterminating company. This time he researched about them on the computer his brother had and learned they specialized in killing vermin that weren't the easiest to get rid of, including the Sydney funnel web spider. The web information didn't give all the details, so he wanted to talk to them to find that out. He also had a second company to do the same with so as to compare which one would be better for him to hire. Because this was an investment of his money, he considered Ralph's suggestions extremely valuable and wise. Because one job was already blown with a death involved, he wanted to make sure that nothing like this ever happened again, at least where he was concerned.

He had brought Sandy for her first day back at school after several days of mourning. Although she seemed fine, he hadn't been sure if she was entirely ready. There were periods of on and off sadness related to the loss of her mother and he didn't want to push the issue of returning to school. Today he hoped it wasn't too soon. When he picked her up at the end of the day, he'd have an inkling of how her day went. Until they returned home, she wouldn't be able to take the school bus, so he would bring her. Maybe for one or two more days the most, he figured.

After he made the two calls, got all the information he needed, and got all the financial figures down, he compared the two. Extermination methods of the funnel web were nearly identical and were nonconventional, which suggested both companies knew what they were doing when it came to dealing with this spider. After he compared the various fees and saw where he could get the best deal, he made his choice and then the call.

#

Sydney, New South Wales

Rodney was there waiting in eager anticipation. He'd gotten there about a half hour early because he wanted to be there when they showed up. This is what he could consider an ultimate and complete house cleansing. It was almost as if the house was demonically haunted. When he looked at the front of it, he wanted so badly to go inside and just continue life as he normally did. He missed it. Yet, knowing what was inside and what had almost gotten him and Friskie made him realize that in order for his return to a normal life, those things had to go. For good. And the people that he knew could destroy them would be here in, now less than thirty minutes. He wasn't about to let those devilish creatures take over his house and home. He'd burn the house down before he let that happen.

He woke up to a tap on his window. Son of a bitch-he had dozed off! Looking out, he saw it was the Gone for Good guys. He got out of the car, and they introduced themselves. Two men in the dark logo'd shirts and pants which identified them with their company.

"Ok, Mr. Johnson, we have the contract here. It states the fees here with a maximum that we can't go over. Whatever fee applies to your house depends on what the assessment shows and the actual work done, as well as how long we spend in there. We can't charge by the hour, but only by the type of work, what it involves, and the level of danger involved. Take a look at it so you'll see what I'm talking about."

Rodney read the two page form with lots of small printing on it. The man called Rob with the shirt bearing his name pointed out what he had just mentioned, then to other areas where he explained and it said it in print that they would not include a charge for the assessment itself. Extermination was in general on the expensive side, but often involved much more work and danger that they could have charged for but didn't. With all things considered, it looked pretty reasonable to Rod. He had no time to pest control hop all over the place. This had to be done, or he'd lose his home, which would be a hell of a lot more of a loss than a couple hundred dollars. He subsequently signed the contract after he was satisfied.

Rob then explained that the assessment might take a couple of hours. He was welcome to sit out here and wait or they could call him if he had other things to do or places to go. They had his number. He agreed to that. Before he left, they assured him that they would check out his crawlspace wearing their special suits and determine the number of locations where the creatures were infiltrating from. If there was only one, then the job could be relatively quick. If there was more, then it could take a little longer. Once they started, it would likely be an all-day task. It would begin tomorrow. He nodded and gave them the key to the front door.

"When you're done, just leave it with my neighbors, the Johnstons. They live next door in that house," Rod explained, pointing to the light blue raised ranch to their left.

"Ok, will do. We'll call you as soon as we're done and let you know our findings."

On that note, Rod left the men to begin what they had to do. He breathed a sigh of relief that it was finally starting. He just hoped nothing would go wrong to jeopardize his return home. His ex-wife Pam used to call him a worry wart for almost worrying about nothing or thinking negative things. But he couldn't help it. Too many things in the past had gone wrong for him or didn't go the way he wanted. However, that wasn't all the time, he admitted to himself. So, he figured he had an alternative if something went wrong here. Plan B. Sell the house if he could. Burning it could put him in jail for arson. He might be slightly extreme in some of his thinking about all this. But he certainly wasn't stupid. It wasn't long before he arrived back at his sister's. The waiting would now continue.

Sydney, New South Wales

Sophie Bloomington had lived in Sydney all her life. At 76, she was on the frail side yet could still get around ok and still drive. Living alone all these years had taken a toll on her, especially since her husband died ten years previously from a heart attack. He'd had a heart condition for some time and she had warned him to stop smoking and ease off on some of the caloric foods he often helped himself to, mostly junk food. He'd been 70 at the time of his death. Despite her warnings, she could only do so much. Although he had been on certain medications, she had to keep on him to remind him to take them when they were due. He wasn't the best in self care, which she figured contributed toward his eventual demise.

Now in her small one bedroom, one story home on the outskirts of the city, she continued her morning chores and rituals. Keeping the kitchen clean, and dusting where necessary were just some of the things which she liked doing because they kept her busy. It was better than just sitting around, knitting like some elderly ladies do. She had decided that wasn't for her because she wasn't that type of person. She needed to keep busy, moving around. If or when the day came around that she was mobility limited and had to sit more, then she'd deal with the knitting part.

She and Charlie had been married for 40 years and had two children together, a boy and a girl. It was the ideal situation for them and they felt they were blessed. Jonathan had grown into a fine young man and was working as an electrical engineer for a large company way out west, just outside of Perth. Julie was the younger of the two siblings by three years and had just graduated from college over in Wellington and was going for her Master's Degree in Economics at the University of Sydney. That pleased Sophie because she could see her daughter every now and then. It would be even better if she could see Jonathan also, but that happened only about three to four times a year. He would fly over either on a job assignment which brought him to this area, or on a vacation or other paid time off schedule.

Despite her age, Sophie didn't look it. She was small and slender, and always managed to keep her hair well coifed. She liked to keep it dark blond and she'd have her hairdresser dye it for her whenever it needed it. In her mind, white didn't become her. Although it wouldn't have mattered to anyone else, it mattered to her. It was one of her most important attributes.

Going along in her cleaning, she liked to hum and sometimes softly sing a few words to some of her favorite songs. Although her home would look spotless to any visitors, she always managed to find some areas that were less than that. For most of her life she'd always had a talent for finding things. Friends knew that and sometimes would kid her by asking her to find something for someone they claimed they couldn't find. Most of the time, she knew, they'd be pulling her leg.

In the living room, she started dusting some of the wooden furniture when her phone rang. Putting down the duster, she answered it which was on one of the end tables near the sofa. It was Julie.

"Hey darlin', what's up? How's school treating ya these days?"

"Doing fine, Mum. Lots of research and stuff, you know how it is. Just calling to see how you're doing and maybe I can come over for a bit this afternoon after classes. Have to study this evening but have a little free time."

"I'm fine. Why sure, come by. Why don't you stay for supper? I'll make your favorite. I have a good cut of pork chops and I already have a nice string bean casserole already made and kept frozen, waiting for the right occasion to warm it up. This sounds like that occasion and we could have it with the chops."

"Great. I can make it. How about 4:30?"

After they agreed, Julie said she had to go. Her next class was coming up. They hung up and then Sophie resumed her cleaning. The humming of the air conditioner seemed to be a soothing sound to her and she continued to listen to it as she dusted around from where she had left off.

It would be another few hours before Julie showed up. Sophie decided to turn on the TV to at least hear voices. It would break up the monotony of silence broken only by the soft humming of the air conditioner. Without that a/c, she'd be roasting inside just as much as outside, if not more.

As she moved around to the other side of the living room, she heard sounds outside her front door. They sounded like the postman was putting mail in her mailbox. Putting down her dusting cloth, she went to the door to retrieve her mail. Behind her on the floor there was movement coming from under the one lounge chair that was there.

Seeing the postman walk away, she greeted him anyway.

"Hi Jack, how are ya?"

"Fine Mrs. Bloomington. And you?"

"Oh ok. Nice day today. You have a good one."

"You too," he replied before getting in his truck and moving over to the next block. Her house had been the last on this one.

Searching through the mail, it was mostly catalogs, and most of them she didn't cater to, so she went and threw most of them away. The one she kept she had decided to look at just for curiosity. An advertising postcard accompanied them and she threw that away. No real mail today. At least there weren't any bills, she thought to herself.

Before resuming her cleaning, she decided to take a brief break by thumbing through the women's catalog she had kept. If she didn't like anything she saw, she'd throw this away also. Sometimes she would find something in those she kept that would peak her interest for possible ordering, especially if she needed something in particular.

She plopped herself down in the lounge chair and started skimming through it, as she listened to some game show that was showing on the TV. There was lots of clapping and cheering and then yelling. Apparently someone had won a huge prize, but she wasn't paying too much attention to it.

When her eye caught something interesting on one of the pages, she felt something brush against the back of her lowermost right leg, just above her shoe. It was almost a tickle but with slightly more pressure. She moved her leg forward a bit in an effort to get rid of that feeling. When she moved her foot back, she bent down to briefly scratch it. That's when she felt the sudden unexpected pain in the back of her hand. It felt like she was being stabbed over and over again, and she yelled out loud. She brought her hand up to look at it, and saw two small droplets of blood on the back of her right hand in line with each other.

The last time she'd felt this much pain she was in labor. It was excruciating beyond description. She looked at her hand with her eyes widened in horror, having difficulty believing what she was seeing. Something had bitten her and she didn't know what. Her hand started swelling right before her eyes, then she felt another sharp sudden pain in her left lowermost leg just above the shoe, which caused her to scream again.

Sophie then knew she was in serious trouble. Something was attacking her and she didn't know what. The pain had taken over to the point where she was no longer aware of the TV or air conditioner sounds. She felt her heart beating rapidly and started sweating. Her hands and arms started shaking and extreme fright accompanied the pain. Groping for the phone, she had a hard time trying to focus on the dial because her hands were shaking so bad.

What she wasn't aware of was that her rapidly beating heart was speeding up the blood running through her veins and arteries. As the blood flow velocity increased, so did the deadly toxin which flowed within the blood itself. Within a minute, the toxin had traveled the full route throughout her body.

As she targeted her shaking index finger on the dial, it became more and more difficult for her to concentrate and control the shaking. Her eyes were so teary from the pain that she had some trouble seeing the dial pad. Her finger hit one number, then another. The breathing difficulties then began and she was starting to fight for air. Another sharp pain on the other lower leg. She found herself nearly unable to move.

As the minutes ticked by, she started becoming less cognizant of her surroundings. Try as she might, it started becoming almost impossible to finish dialing the number she had started. Her body was wracked entirely by agonizing pain, now considerably worse than any childbirth pain. She sank down in the chair screaming for help. No one outside could hear her from inside the house.

Her vision started to double and she had to fight for every breath. She contorted in the chair as if trying to somehow ease the pain that seemed to be more severe in some areas than others. She was now unaware of her profusely swollen right hand, now appearing as if it was a blown up balloon. There was no longer any control she had of herself, and her bladder let go. For several more minutes, she cried out in agony for help that would never come in time.

For all of her married life, she swore that if anything ever happened to Charlie, she would never let him pass away alone. She would be there with him and for him and to reassure him that she loved him always and forever, and she would see him again up in heaven. She promised him that before he died. When he did finally succumb, which was fairly quickly, he seemed to be at peace with that and seeing her with him for the last time.

Now here, she was alone. She knew she was going to die, and she would die alone. She became weak. Her eyes were full of tears, more from the sadness of leaving this world in the company of no one and not able to see her children anymore at least in this world. She could feel the life draining out of her as her organs started shutting down. Her blood pressure dropped dramatically as her heart actually increased considerably in its beat, trying to make up for the lost pressure. It would soon fail, as her body went into shock.

She became unconscious. Her blood, now filled with deadly venom, inundated her brain with its destructive chemicals. Even if help had arrived at this time, it would be far too late to save her. Sophie Bloomington died alone at home. The time was 11:47am.

Hours ticked by until her daughter showed up. When Julie came in the door, she saw almost immediately her mother lying on the floor. Her left arm was alongside of her, but her right arm was stretched out. She started quickly to move toward her, then stopped dead in her tracks with a look of horror suddenly etched on her face. Her eyes were widened as they took in the sight. Still she called out. "Mom. Mom are you alright?" She couldn't believe what she was seeing.

The three large spiders walked slowly from her arm and then onto her chest. Her mom never answered her.

She called out to her mother again in an act of desperation, hoping beyond hope that her mother would say something. But she neither said anything nor moved. Julie saw a complete absence of her chest rising and lowering. Her mother's right hand was all blown up, the areas around her ankles were swollen almost beyond belief, and she saw a bluish tinge on her face. Julie was suddenly hit with the realization that she was dead.

There was no way she was going further into the house. She saw all that she needed to see. Backing out, she took out her cell phone and called for an ambulance and the police, telling the emergency operator what she saw. In tears and crying almost uncontrollably, she didn't know who else to call, but they would figure it out once they saw for themselves. It was difficult for her to talk because of her crying, as with most traumatized witnesses. But once she got out the word *spiders,* the emergency operator was already contacting the nearest entomologist contracted with the region's authorities, in addition to paramedics and police.

Sadly, the creatures had claimed yet another victim. It didn't take long for Sophie Bloomington's death to hit the airwaves. Even more people were on the alert now and just as many scared to even be in their houses. What would they find in their shoes or closets, or under any of the furniture? What was happening nearly caused an epidemic of paranoia as people now eyed all dark places as if a terrible monster would come out and get them. It was a fear never before experienced, neither in Sydney nor anywhere else. Entomologists everywhere were scrambling to find out why this terrifying epidemic of funnel webs was occurring.

They all wondered basically the same thing: the reason for it, were they coming from a particular nest and if so where was it? They needed to keep track of the exact locations of these attacks and try to determine a geographical pattern. Were these attacks in one particular area of the city and surrounding suburbs or were they spread everywhere haphazardly in no particular pattern? If it was the former, then they could set up what police would call a perimeter and try to rid the area of them all at once. If it was the latter, then the solution would be considerably more problematic.

The regional government subsequently brought together scientists in entomology and arachnoid specialists to work on this and figure out a solution as quickly as possible before people started panicking. That's the last thing anyone wanted to happen. As with everything else, it would take a little time to get things started. Unlike everything else, it was happening a little quicker than normal.

December 12, University of Sydney, New South Wales

Mary Welling had heard enough. After hearing, reading, and seeing a number of reports of unusual funnel web occurrences and attacks that were far beyond the normal, even for this region and now the most recent death, she decided to try and spread the word about these things and prevention methods. The best way to spread the word was through the media, especially television.

Contacting the local station for the Sydney area, she explained why she was calling and identified herself as the expert that she was. After realizing she could provide valuable information to the public regarding this outbreak, the person on the other end asked her to hold for a moment. Mary was sensing she was going to contact either a supervisor to ok whatever they were going to ok, or a reporter. When she came back on the phone a couple of minutes later, it was the latter.

A reporter could show up in an hour to her office at the school if she chose. Mary readily agreed to that. She hoped her attempt to warn and advise people would help and perhaps lessen the chances of more people becoming victims. If she had been responsible for the spread of these creatures because of an accident in her lab a couple of months earlier, she wanted to at least try to redeem herself however she could and make things go back to normal again.

She knew, of course, that it could never be known for sure if that accident and the escape of an unknown number of funnel web spiderlings from her lab was responsible for this outbreak and subsequent attacks on people. For legal and wise reasons, she couldn't admit to something if she didn't really know if it was true or not. That could open a Pandora's Box unnecessarily. The last thing she wanted was to create a scenario of misperceptions and needless finger-pointing. Best to not say anything about that, she concluded. Her decision to provide expert advice in combating the current situation and also publicize prevention methods was the best way she could help the situation improve.

As a matter of appropriate etiquette and protocol, she contacted Dean Minson to let him know what she planned on doing. Although he was slightly leery of her plan primarily because it was the media she would be talking to, she assured him that she would not get the school or the department involved, and that she only wanted to give advice to the public as an expert. The dean warned her she could not speak on behalf of the school or state what she thought was its opinions, although she stated she should mention the school name if asked for it. That was to give credibility to her as an expert in this field of entomology. In the end, he agreed.

She also let Ted know what she was going to do and when the interview would take place, so she would be uninterrupted. She let her secretary know to hold all calls from such and such a time until the interview was completed. Her next class wasn't until this evening at 7, so she had the afternoon free, which made it perfect. It was 2:00 pm now. She had an hour to prepare both what she would say and would not say. She'd spoken to the media before and realized one had to be careful what one said. Saying the wrong thing or saying something which could easily be perceived in more than one way, especially to a reporter, could end up being misquoted or broadcast in a way that sent the wrong message. She positioned herself at her desk and started her preparations.

The phone then rang. "Hello, Professor Welling," she answered.

It was Dean Minson. "Hi Mary, John here. I just got a call from the mayor's office, believe it or not. Not the usual phone call I get. Apparently it has to do with the latest incidents with these spiders and from the latest death. You heard?"

"Yes, as a matter of fact, I just heard this morning. So why's the mayor calling you?"

"Well, we are getting together a small group of entomologists to try to handle and solve this problem which seems to be getting worse.

There's a couple of arachnologists named in the bunch, and you happen to be one of them."

"Me? Are you kidding? And who's we?"

"Of course you. Why not? We include the university and the National Department of Entomology."

"But there are other arachnologists around."

"Sure there are, Mary. But none of them have the specialized expertise you have with the Sydney Funnel Web. Face it. You are needed and non-expendable. That should be a bit of a feather in your cap, I should say."

Mary looked down and rubbed her forehead. She wasn't sure if she wanted to do this or not. But it seemed she didn't have a choice.

"Does that mean working there, wherever there is, versus here?"

"You'll be working full time with the group. You can check on your lab here when you have the time. But your priority will be to help solve this problem which you know is only worsening."

"What? Wait a minute John, I can't do that. What about all my classes? I'm already going on TV, I have term papers to correct, important research I've been continuing on, meetings I'm supposed to be conducting, and my out of town conference I'm scheduled to attend week after next."

"Do what you have to do to reschedule. I'll get a proper substitute for your classes, beginning the day after tomorrow. You can figure out yourself when you can correct the term papers. But this is an emergency situation and your help is very much needed. Get your secretary to help you in whatever you need."

"Ok. I'll take care of it. But where and when will we be getting together?"

"Thursday. Nine am in the Lindsey building conference room."

"Who's running this thing?"

"A man named Robertson. Doctor Eric Robertson from the University of Brisbane. He's had experience with a few heavy infestations in his time. Mainly other types of spiders and other bugs."

"But none of this type?" Mary interjected.

"Of course not. Have you ever heard of any other funnel web invasions such as this?"

Mary had to admit she hadn't.

"I thought not," the dean replied. "So this will be a first. For all of you. But since he's got the invasion experience, he gets to lead the way here; however, under your strict guidance. However, this may not be as much of a field trip as more of a think tank."

"Oh?"

"Yes, well as I understand it, certain extermination companies with experience and expertise in getting rid of these particular creatures seem to have been taking care of the problem so far. One of the houses infested they hosed down the crawlspace under the house where these creatures had a huge funnel web nest. Other houses were found to have the same thing. So these expert fellows will be contracted and funded, courtesy of the City of Sydney, to rid any homes of these things, at no cost to the residents. Your group will be figuring out why this has happened and perhaps prevent this from occurring again. Anyway, that's the scoop."

The conference room where they were to meet was in the main administration building. She had been there twice before for special conferences. "Ok, then, I'll be there. I better get going and start getting my things in order here."

After they hung up, Mary contacted her secretary and let her know the news. She'd be gone for an undetermined amount of time but would keep in touch when she could so she would be kept in the loop regarding her students and how they were faring with the substitute.

Gathering her things, she left to grab a coffee in the cafeteria. There was a class she had later that afternoon, then a couple tomorrow. She decided to announce her temporary reassignment to her classes, leaving out unnecessary details. It could be for the rest of the semester, she would add, but they had a perfectly qualified substitute who was also an entomologist that they could count on for instruction and help. This was Dean Minson's idea, so she knew that if there were any problems, it would be on him to resolve them. But then again, he had always been reliable in finding the right people for the job so she was confident that the substitute would be a good one, she thought as she sipped her coffee, then broke out one of the term papers she'd brought with her. No time like the present to get started on this.

#

December 12, Goulburn, New South Wales

On this hot, summer Saturday, six-year-old Penny Worthington was outside in her backyard playing with her friend Nickie from next door. Both girls were wearing their bathing suits. For them, it was nice and fun using the small round pool where they could frolic in the cool water for as long as they could or get in and out whenever they wanted. Both were playing with the rubber ball, playing catch in the pool.

Nickie was just a year older than Penny and slightly taller. While Penny was blonde and green-eyed like her mom Wanda, Nickie had the brown hair and eyes that was a reflection of both her parents. They were best friends and loved to play together when they could. It didn't happen every day but they didn't complain about that.

"C'mon, Nickie. Throw it. I'm ready." Penny held her hands up as they both sat in the pool and Nickie was ready to throw the ball to her friend. When she did, she underestimated the power of her throw because it went over Penny's head, rolled over the lawn and stopped at the edge of a patch of brush settling into a slight depression in the ground.

"You threw it too far, Nickie," said Penny as she got up, turned, and climbed out of the pool to run after the ball.

"I'm sorry." Penny heard behind her.

When Penny got to the brush edge, at first she didn't see the ball. She looked around in the thick brush which could easily hide even a large ball. Eventually she found it and saw it was in a little gulley. Thinking nothing of it, she picked it up and saw a hole where the ball had been. She'd never seen a hole like that before and wondered how it got there. She also saw something sticking out of it and when she felt it, it felt like a silky thread in her hand. A piece of it, from the looks of it, she thought.

When she looked a little closer at the hole, she saw what looked like a white tunnel.

"Hey, I found something here," Penny yelled out to her friend.

While Nickie clambered out of the pool, without any thought but with plenty of curiosity of a young child, Penny got on her hands and knees to peer more closely at the mysterious hole. With the child's typical lack of danger awareness and caution, she inserted the tips of her fingers through the hole entrance. Feeling more of the silky thread inside the hole, she thought it felt pretty strange. She'd never seen or felt anything like this before.

When Nickie arrived to where Penny was, she asked, "What are you doing?"

"I'm feeling a funny string in here. I feel it move but it feels funny."

"Funny like crazy string?" asked Nickie, referring to the canned string sold in toy stores or toy departments.

"No, silly. Like stringy string." She kept wiggling her fingers inside and felt a small piece of it come off. Pulling her fingers out of the hole, both girls looked at the white, thread-like string piece in her fingers.

"Ooo, what's string doing in a hole in the ground?" Nickie looked at it more closely in Penny's fingers.

Penny shrugged. "I don't know. Maybe I could pull some more out."

"No," Nickie objected. "You better not. Maybe there's a big snake down there or some kind of monster."

"Don't be silly," retorted Penny. "Monsters don't live in holes in the ground. And we don't have any snakes around here."

Penny stuck her fingers back in there then pushed half of her little hand in there trying to get more of it out. Unfortunately, the further in her hand went, the smaller and tighter the hole became and the "funny string" around it. Her hand became stuck when she tried to pull it out.

"Oh, no, my hand is stuck." Penny started to cry. She kept pulling but her hand was positioned so she couldn't open it inside the hole. It was scrunched in there. When she tried to pull it out, she couldn't.

"Nickie, help me I can't get my hand out." Penny was crying out loud.

When Nickie tried to pull on Penny to maybe help her get her hand out of the hole, it only seemed to make her friend cry harder. Inside the hole, Penny felt the string wiggle against her hand continuously, although her fingers were scrunched together so tightly that she couldn't have moved them to move the string if she wanted to. Something else was moving the string.

Suddenly Penny let out a bloodcurdling scream that not only terrified Nickie, but made her cry as well. Penny didn't know what it was, but she had felt a severe, knife-like burning pain in her hand that hurt more than anything else she felt in her life. She screamed so loud, the neighbors came out. Ron and Wanda, Penny's parents came running out as quickly as they could. They knew it was Penny and something very bad had happened. Nickie was crying fiercely, afraid for her friend who was screaming at the top of her lungs in agony. Her hand was still stuck in the hole and the stabbing pains and burning continued and worsened.

When Ron went to Penny and immediately saw her hand was stuck in some kind of hole, Wanda took Nickie in her arms and comforted her while Ron helped their daughter. Penny's face was beet red in her expressions of agony. Inside the hole, the stabbings continued. Ron pounded the hole and dug at it, doing everything he could to allow Penny's hand to come out of there. Finally it did.

The hand was covered in dirt, and white thread fibers. Attached to the fibers that he had pulled out with Penny's hand was a large, black spider. His jaw dropped and his eyes widened in fear; fear not for the dead spider but for what was happening to his daughter. He looked at her. Her crying had stopped but her eyes had rolled up into her head. Muscular twitching appeared on various areas of her body, and he noticed some drooling at her mouth. She was unconscious.

Knowing what he had to do as a chief paramedic for the Canberra Ambulance Company, he tore off his shirt and applied immediate pressure to Penny's hand.

"Wanda, call emergency services immediately. Tell them we need an ambulance as soon as they can get here. Yesterday if possible!"

"Ron, what is it?" Wanda was in tears now along with poor Nickie.

"Tell them Penny's been bitten by a funnel web spider. The Sydney one. Possibly multiple bites. I dragged a dead one out with her hand. Go!"

Taking Nickie with her, Wanda ran into the house and called the emergency services. It was what would be considered a Priority One, meaning if help didn't arrive within the next ten to fifteen minutes, the victim could die.

As he kept the pressure on her hand, the hand was quickly swelling up as antibodies rushed to the site of envenomation to fight the inner battle of body versus invader. The deadly venom coursed through the little girl's body and could quickly overtake her body's systems. Because she was small, the time to save her would be shorter than for an adult. Ron kept the pressure on her hand and would not release her hand until his colleagues took over.

The neighbors on the other side of the Worthington house from where Nickie's house was came over to see what was wrong and if they could help in any way. When they saw what was happening and what had happened to little Penny, they were horrified.

"Oh my God, Ron. Oh Jeez, can we do anything, anything at all for you?" asked Sam Monohan. He'd always been a good neighbor so it wasn't a surprise to see him there first.

"No, thank you Sam. Wanda just called for an ambulance."

"Is she going to be alright?"

"I don't know. Fifty-fifty right now. She's been bitten by the Sydney funnel web spider."

The Monohans' faces both expressed shock at the same time. "Oh dear Lord, how did that happen?" asked Sam's wife, Millie.

Before he could answer, Wanda came out of the house. "They'll be here in five minutes. They're coming here at top speed. They've also called for the MedFlight helicopter which is leaving Sydney now."

For Ron, five minutes seemed like an eternity. Right now, Penny's life was draining away and he was doing all that he could to prevent the end for her. This was not fair. No child should die. Especially like this.

Then Nickie's mother came over. Taking Nickie from Wanda, she spoke to Wanda while the women looked over to where Ron was leaning over their daughter. Nickie's mother was just as horrified and nearly in tears as well when she found out. What happened to Penny could very well have been *her* daughter instead. But she was just as frightened for Penny as she would have been for Nickie.

Ron looked down at her still unconscious daughter. She was still breathing. He tied a tourniquet around her wrist as soon as he had someone find some material for him. Sam had removed his T-shirt, ripped a long piece off of it and handed it to Ron.

"Here, Ron. Maybe you'll want this."

Ron took it gratefully. It wasn't a cure and certainly wouldn't end this horror, but it could buy them time to save her life.

Soon the ambulance came with medics running to them with their equipment and stretcher as fast as they could. "Chopper is on the way and should be here within the next two or three minutes," one of them yelled as they neared their patient on the ground.

When they got to Ron and Penny, they quickly assessed the situation. "We got it." Ron let go and the medics saw the tourniquet and took over. They immediately took Penny's vital signs. As one took it, he spoke out the readings. "BP 65 over 35, AP 150." Sandwiching the end of one of her fingers between two clasps, they waited for the reading on that electronic device, which came quickly. SAT 93 it said. They removed the devices and contacted the medics on the approaching chopper with the information. Then they connected an IV to her and hooked her up to normal saline for hydration and hopefully provide some dilution to the venom's potency.

What the readings were telling them was that Penny's blood pressure was lower than it should be while her heart rate was way too fast. With the number they read, it would be even for an adult. Her blood oxygen level was 93. Normal is 98-100. So Penny was suffering also from oxygen deprivation. Anti-venom was already ordered to be ready on Penny's arrival at Sydney hospital.

The chopper arrived on the Worthington's front lawn. After Penny was quickly put on the stretcher, she was whisked away toward the helicopter. Neighbors from all around the neighborhood were now outside watching the scenario unfolding before them. No helicopter, even MedFlight, had ever landed here before. They knew it was pretty serious and wanted to find out what happened. Fortunately, they held back from approaching the scene until a more appropriate time. Soon the chopper was off. In ten minutes, Penny would arrive and hopefully with answered prayers, she would be saved. It was all anyone could do right now. With each minute that passed, the venom was destroying her insides, bringing her closer to death.

23

December 12, Sydney Memorial Hospital, Sydney, Australia

In the ER, doctors and nurses were already waiting for Penny to arrive. Their exam area was already prepared for her arrival. The anti-venom had been ordered and delivered from their special storage locker. An attending physician who specialized in anti-venom treatments was on hand already. He had been treating a few other patients who'd received venomous bites, one from a brown snake and two others from a funnel web. All three were adults. This would be the first child that appeared here for such a case.

When Penny arrived, they wasted no time in preparing her for the necessary treatment. They noticed a lot of drooling from her mouth and tears coming from her eyes: two of the signs of systemic envenomation by this spider. In addition, she was in and out of consciousness and, when conscious, exhibited severe malaise, which was another definite sign of the envenomation. As if those were not enough, she was also showing muscle twitching which were continuous all over her body with some involuntary muscle ripplings, especially in her thighs. Something like that would be impossible to do voluntarily which usually meant a severe toxin crisis which, in turn, could worsen at any moment into a generalized convulsion. That also would increase her risk of death.

Treatment had to be started as soon as possible because if pulmonary edema developed, which was very likely if no preventive measures were taken, Penny's risk of dying would be doubled from what it already was. She was basically teetering on the edge of death right now. The pulmonary edema would likely put her over the edge and kill her.

Children were more likely to die and die more quickly than adults from the Sydney funnel web spider bite. The medical team had to work fast and prepare to infuse the appropriate anti-venom as quickly as possible. Time was not on their side. Because of her age and size, they had to calculate precisely how much of the toxic solution to give the young girl based on her weight in kilograms. Any deviation from that would affect the outcome. Too much of it would kill her. Too little of it would make it ineffective and allow the venom to continue its destructive course. While some of the medical staff was preparing her, the attending ER physician was making sure everything was prepared for a possible anaphylactic reaction to the anti-venom. Although it was rare with this particular one, exclusive only for funnel web spider bites, it was still possible in some patients. If this were to happen with Penny, she would suddenly develop a significant drop in blood pressure or bronchospasm. Should that occur, they would have to temporarily stop the anti-venom treatment and give her subcutaneous injections of prescribed amounts of adrenaline, plus 100% oxygen.

There were two attending ER physicians on the case. The one trained and certified in anti-venom treatments was Dr. Michael Boller, who'd been on the medical staff there for fifteen years and had been certified in and sub-specialized in medical anti-venom treatments for seven of those years. He was highly successful and known for his occasional off-beat treatments which he used when all conventional methods failed. Surprisingly and fortunately for him and the patients, he was rewarded with more successes for his efforts than not.

The other physician, Dr. Jonathan Pullman, had been there for about ten years and was training as a fellow under the supervision of Dr. Boller. Together they were readying to work on Penny and pull her through this critical crisis. It would not be easy, which seemed to be the way it always was with insect or spider envenomation.

"Ok, are we ready?" asked Dr. Boller. He saw the IV port and small tube sticking from one of her arm veins. That had already been flushed with a normal saline solution to ensure unimpeded access of the anti-venom solution.

He had ordered six bottles to be there. Two were extras if needed. Because of Penny's severe envenomation, he chose to treat her with a total of four vials instead of the usual two. Each of the vials were child specific and were thus smaller in size. The adrenaline was ready just in case. Fortunately, anaphylactic reactions rarely occurred with the CSL funnel web spider anti-venom because of a certain medical effect of the venom which didn't occur in other types of spider venoms: the only positive thing about this venom, if one can call it that.

Two nurses stood by Penny's side, monitoring her closely. Penny was hooked up to the vital sign monitor which hung from the wall. It showed her blood pressure, respiration, heart rate, and blood saturation level. An alarm would go off if any of the readings became abnormally high or low. They had to watch it very carefully. Penny was also hooked up to an EKG monitor so they could continuously monitor the heart readings for any abnormalities which could occur at any time.

Quickly the hanging bottle was connected by the tubing to the IV port, the port was opened up, the clamp to the solution was opened up and the solution started running into her vein. Another hydrating solution was opened and running into a secondary port next to the anti-venom one. She had to be monitored continuously at all times throughout the administering of all four bottles. It would be touch and go because on some people these treatments didn't work and they would die anyway.

As the treatment began, Penny's parents had just arrived at the hospital, asking for their daughter. Hospital personnel helped them and brought them back to the treatment room where Penny was. Wanda was in tears, and Ron was fighting as hard as he could to keep it together for Wanda's sake. Despite his efforts, his eyes became tear-saturated when they saw their daughter hooked up to several tubes, a urinary catheter attached to a bag hanging beside the bed, wires connected to cardiac and respiratory monitors, and an oxygen mask covering half her face. They saw two IV drips going into her. One was a large bag, and the other a bottle of something unknown to them. One of the doctors informed them that it was the anti-venom in the bottle and that the other in the bag was a normal saline solution to keep her hydrated and her kidneys flushed. He was compassionate in his explanation of everything they needed to know and to ensure they were doing everything they possibly and humanly could to save her life. For them, it was heartbreaking to see their six-year-old girl for the first time wired and tubed all over the place, unconscious, and fighting for her young life. For the moment, they could only pray and hope He would listen. It would be many hours that would pass before anyone would know if she pulled through or not. They had all the time in the world to pray.

24

December 12, Canberra, New South Wales

As arranged the previous day, Peter met the exterminators around 10:00 am at his house. They were from the company he chose who were reputable in the area and were known to be highly successful in their funnel web kill missions, as Peter thought of them. Unbeknownst to him, someone else not far away had also hired them around the same time for the same problem, and there were probably others as well. They had said in their conversation that they were kept busy within the last couple of weeks especially. "Lots of these things appearing, I'm afraid," he had told Peter.

"But we get called and hired, we get rid of them, and people are happy. We make sure that they are gone for good. Hence, our name. So here's the plan, Mr. Ingram."

As their colleagues had done with Rodney, the man called John did the same with him. After Peter had read and signed the contract, the assessment could be done. Treatment would be by water and not chemicals. There would be some flooding in the basement, he explained. After they had destroyed the nest with high-pressure water hosing and all spiders that were in it, they would search the entire house, from top to bottom. They would not flood the house if they saw any on the upper floors. They would physically kill them if they could by more primitive methods if there was only one or two. More than that, they had a plan to lure them down to the basement.

Once they had cleared out or made sure all the upper floors had no spiders or nests, they would do a recheck in the basement area, including all hard to see or hard to get to areas. They wouldn't begin the final treatment process until they were 100 per cent sure that there were no nests or spiders left.

Once that was done, they would drain out all the water in the basement with a special pump that they'd bring in. All creatures and the destroyed nests would be completely cleaned out of there. All webbing of any sort would be removed.

The price for all this was not just financial. Any things that were left around that couldn't be removed from there, which was just about anything that could hide spiders or other crawlies, would likely be permanently damaged by the treatment. They wanted to make sure that

Peter understood this would be an all or nothing job. If he wanted his home back completely spider free, including other less harmful species, then unfortunately this would likely occur.

Peter understood and agreed. He didn't want another death and he wanted his home back. Things could easily be replaced. On that note and mutual understanding, he left the men to do their job, along with his cell phone number. They'd call him when the all day job was done.

#

December 13, University of Sydney, New South Wales

Mary Welling's interview with the reporter had gone pretty well. They asked her if she could appear for a three-minute segment on tomorrow's news broadcast at 12 noon. She readily agreed, but also letting them know right off the bat that she wouldn't offer any opinions of the university or her department. This was strictly her idea and desire to inform the public what they should know regarding this outbreak and possibly with the results of preventing further injuries or fatalities. After the reporter agreed and left to return to her stations, Mary sat wondering if she was doing the right thing. How could it not be the right thing? When she remembered what could have caused this outbreak, again she became convinced of it and this was what she needed to do. A knock on her door suddenly interrupted her thoughts.

She opened it to a female student who looked like she wasn't sure if she should be there.

"I'm sorry to interrupt you, Professor."

"No, no, that's quite alright. I just finished a chat session and was going to open the door anyway. What can I do for you?"

"I'm in your entomology 101 class on Mondays and Wednesdays. I just heard some news from friends of my parents and since you're a specialist in spiders, thought you'd want to know."

Mary looked at her curiously wondering what news she had that might make her interested.

"What's your name, if I may ask?"

"Oh, I'm sorry," she replied with a smile. "I'm Brenda. Brenda Wiley. Sorry about that."

"That's ok, Brenda. I think I remember you. You're the student that asks lots of questions. Interesting ones, I should add."

"Yes, I am," Brenda said giggling. "Thank you for the interesting part."

"Anyway, what news would you like to share with me? Oh, come in. Have a seat there," Mary indicated by pointing at the chair beside her desk. Brenda sat down.

"Well I can't stay long. Anyway, as I said my parents have friends over in Goulburn. I know them too. Their daughter just got bitten apparently multiple times by an Atrax."

Mary's eyes bored into the girl's. "Really? How old is she?"

"Six."

"Six years old?"

"Yes. She's in the Sydney hospital ER right now. From what I heard she's in bad shape. They're working on her right now. I haven't been able to get there, but my folks found out about it and I guess are at the hospital with her parents now."

This was clearly disturbing to Mary. A child! Even getting appropriate treatment in a rapid amount of time might still not be enough to save her, because of her small size, still somewhat weak immune system, and the fact that she received multiple bites. How horrible can that be for *anyone*, let alone a child?

"How did that happen? Was it in her house?"

"No," Brenda replied. Then she went on to explain the events in the backyard that eventually led to the biting.

"Well, I won't keep you, Professor. Thanks for your time," said Brenda, getting up to leave.

"Thank you for the information, Brenda. I appreciate that. Keep me posted about the little girl. What's her name?"

"Penny."

"Would you keep me updated about her, please? I'd really like to know."

Brenda smiled at her. "I sure will. I'll let you know the minute I find out."

Before she left, Mary handed over her business card. "Here's my card and number. Leave a message if I'm not here. I always listen to my voicemails when I get back to the office."

The co-ed agreed and was gone, en route to wherever she had to go. Mary shuffled some papers on her desk. She couldn't help thinking about the poor little girl and couldn't imagine how awful the parents might be feeling at that moment. Although there was nothing she could do or be of any help for the ongoing circumstances, now she felt more than ever that her appearance on television about all this was not only the right thing to do but the necessary thing as well.

25

December 13, Canberra, New South Wales

Back in his house, Peter sighed with relief that it was done. He thought about having gotten the call that the job was finished. He couldn't help feeling a little apprehensive because of the two tragedies that had happened in his house. Did this treatment, this extermination work? Did they really get rid of these things? At this point, he didn't really care about any damage to things left in the basement. All he wanted was for his home to be pest free. Spider free, whether it be this funnel web type or other types. He wanted them *all* gone. After what happened, he didn't trust any of them. Not being an entomologist, he considered them all scary looking and therefore they were all potentially deadly.

The exterminators had asked him to come inside where they met in the living room at the front of the house. They were very good not only in their work but in the way they explained it all.

"This is what we did. And it was everything we told ya beforehand. Downstairs is a complete cleanout and washout. It's a little wet but you won't find any evidence of any more of those things. For the previous guys who didn't have the right weapons, it was not having water pure and simple that was the ticket to their demise. Water in the right place where they nested. That's what kills them. They didn't do what they should have done. Lucky the one made it."

Then he went on to explain what else they did.

"We checked all the floors upstairs and here. There were no rovers that we could see, no spaces that we saw. Under things, over things, beside things, in closets, checked for holes anywhere, spaces, cracks, and crevices they might hide or have webs. Nothing. Did this in every room on every floor. Even checked the drains in the bathroom and kitchen sink. Anywhere where it could be dark. Especially downstairs which had more of all those areas than anywhere else in the house. And especially under and behind the washer and dryer, and all around the furnace. There wasn't one square inch of floor and along the ceiling edges where we didn't find anything. When we checked for an attic, we didn't find one, cause we forgot to ask you."

"No, I don't have one, thank God. Is just as well. Anyway sounds like you guys did as thorough a job as can be done."

Then they had taken him down to see the basement. John was intelligent enough to know that sometimes returning to areas where tragedy had occurred could be emotionally difficult for people, and felt he had to ask. Although Peter didn't really want to go down there ever again, if he wanted his home back he'd have to.

Going down there was difficult for him. He'd known it would be. At the bottom of the stairs is where his wife's body had been found. This was where the creatures had ambushed and attacked her. This is where she had died an agonizing death. What made it even worse was the fact that she had been alone at the time.

It was horrible and he found himself in a near panic attack. The memories came flooding back to him uncontrollably and he wished right at that moment he was anywhere but here. His rapid breathing and near nervous breakdown disturbed the exterminators so much, they decided they needed to get him back upstairs now.

Back in the living room, they waited to see if he would settle down.

"Are you alright, mate? Want a drink of water?" the other man, Steve, asked.

Peter shook his head, with his breathing now starting to slow down. He'd never experienced anything like that before. It was horrible. A panic attack? If it was, he never wanted to experience that again, ever.

"I'm sorry, gentlemen. I didn't mean for that to happen. I had no idea."

"That's ok, Mr. Ingram. Perfectly understandable." John was concerned. He'd never seen a reaction like that in anyone, in clients with some of the worst cases. But then none of the others had two deaths occur soon after the other in virtually the same spot in the same house. So he could say that Peter Ingram's case was quite unique but terrible enough for no one to ever want it repeated again.

"You sure you're ok? We can call someone for you if you like?"

"No, thank you," Peter said, looking down at the floor in embarrassment. "I'll be ok. I have family and friends I can call."

John nodded. "Ok. Now, just know that the house is thoroughly clean. Downstairs, we blocked off all cracks, crevices, and spaces that could lead something from other areas. Nothing will get through those blocks, not even those bloody funnel webs. We did all we could to ensure nothing like that happens again."

"I appreciate all you did. What do I owe you?"

John took out the paperwork from his folder and explained the different costs. In the end, it did sound pricey initially. But when you looked at everything they did, including above and beyond what they were hired for, it turned out to be a bargain, especially when it came to them fortifying the entire house against future encroachments of these deadly creatures.

"If you ever find something like this getting in again, call us right away. We'll check it out. If it turns out to be another funnel web that somehow got through the blockade, we'll get rid of it at no charge. If it's something else you want us to rid you of, then applicable fees will apply to that. If it's something you can handle, better to do it that way. Can save you a lot of money."

Peter took his advice and as they stood up, they shook hands and soon the men were gone. His house was clean. They couldn't have reassured him more than they did. He might have to do his laundry at the Laundromat for a while. His fear for going downstairs was understandably real and he didn't know whether he'd ever be able to go down there again. For the time being, he decided he and Sandy could move back in and restart their lives without Tabitha.

26

December13, 8:00am, Wollongong, New South Wales

They were going to work on the house yesterday but there was a glitch. Their main service truck had sprung a leak in one of the engine hoses and had to be repaired before they could use it. Once the one day delay was over, Rodney had been told that's all they could do today. Their initial task was to first permanently repair the hole in the closet wall so there'd no longer be any access for the spiders or anything else to get into the house. Once the wall was repaired and there were no more holes to be seen anywhere, they would again check the entire house, in every room everywhere for the creatures. The attic would be the first place they'd start and work down. In fact, even if it started early this morning, it would take the entire day to do what they did. If they couldn't get done by the end of the day, they'd finish tomorrow. Charges would be for the completed job and what was involved, not by the day.

After he let them in, he left to go to work. He didn't want to take time off just for this. Besides, they needed him to not be there while they did what they needed to do there. There might be some chemicals used to kill other kinds of bugs they saw along the way. For this reason, Rodney kept Friskie at Celia's until his home was readied to move back into. Hopefully that would happen by the end of the day. But if it had to be tomorrow, that was ok, as long as those devilish creatures were gone for good.

10:00am, Sydney Memorial Hospital, New South Wales

The second bottle of anti-venom had been given the evening before and they now started her on the third bottle. Penny's vitals seemed to settle down a bit, but were still out of the normal range for her age and size. Her blood pressure was still below normal although slightly higher than it was, and her heart rate was above a normal rate still. That didn't change, so she was still far from being out of the woods.

As her parents watched with nervous apprehension, she appeared in and out of consciousness. The nurses had given her pain medication and some Ativan to help with some of the anxiety and muscle twitching. Every once in a while, even during her sedated state, her face would grimace. When Wanda asked the nurse why she kept doing that every so often, the answer was chilling.

"Mrs. Worthington, the pain she's going through is beyond description. Even though she's sedated and has been given strong pain medications, the pain from the venom is so powerful, that it can even come through some of those meds. That's why she's grimacing. If she didn't have those meds in her system, her screams would be continuous and piercing probably beyond what you ever heard before. That's not something she should ever endure, nor should you or anyone else have to hear them."

Wanda was in tears again and Ron put his arm around her in a measure of comfort. Although he seemed a tad stoic about this, Wanda would know that what was happening to their little girl was emotionally killing him. He was trying his best to be strong about this for Wanda's sake but he was finding it more and more difficult to not break out into tears.

As the minutes and then hours ticked by, all kinds of thoughts went through Wanda's mind. First it was about her daughter and what was happening to her inside and if she would pull through or not; then she wondered as the nurses and doctors came in and out to check on her frequently how they could see patients in distress every day, especially children like her daughter without being emotionally and psychologically affected. She knew she couldn't do something like this, but she was grateful that they could.

During the second hour, an ER technician would come in to check Penny's urinary output in the bag and record it down. The nurse would come in to check the running of the continuous IV of normal saline and then the anti-venom. She then also had to record down the vital signs and any observations noted related to its infusion. Whenever the doctor finished on the computer out there in the main nurses' station, he'd come back in to check on Penny.

"Doctor, what do you think? Think this third bottle is doing anything yet?" Wanda was both nervous and impatient. The doctor knew it but he understood because her daughter's life was hanging in the balance right now.

"Mrs. Worthington, so far she seems to be stable. Because we've been able to put her on the third bottle, that's a good sign. It means she doesn't seem to be allergic to it. So we have dodged a bullet there. But she's not out of the woods."

"Well, when might you know when...."

Suddenly, Penny's body went into violent jerking and then what appeared to be a full body convulsion. It was the classic tonic-clonic episode of a grand mal seizure.

The doctor ran to the wall and pressed the large red button, then yelled out loud. "Code Blue, Code Blue, ER, 12." Suddenly all kinds of medical staff came running in, including one with a crash cart 30 seconds later.

Wanda screamed, terrified at the sight before her. Her daughter was thrashing in bed with a violence she'd never seen in anyone.

"Mrs. Worthington, does your daughter have epilepsy or a seizure disorder?" asked Dr. Gray who was the physician attending her.

Wanda who was in tears now yelled out. "No! No! She never had anything like that. What's happening? What's happening to my daughter?"

"Oh my God!" Ron yelled out in fear.

Sam Gray told one of the nurses to quietly and quickly escort the parents back outside the exam room, preferably to a waiting area. As a doctor, he really didn't want hysterical parents screaming which could be distracting in a life-threatening situation. In the meantime, he started barking out orders. Because she was a child, he had to be extra cautious regarding how much medication to give her, especially in regards to administering a dangerous antitoxin. Children couldn't be given meds the same way as adults.

"How much does she weigh? Find out from the mother."

One of the nurses ran out. She came back within seconds. "43 pounds."

The doctor quickly calculated into kilograms and ordered the appropriate dosage of Ativan IV according to her kilogram weight. Calculations like this were necessary only for children, not adults, when it came to determining medication dosage. He ordered 0.5 milligrams of the anxiety and antispasmodic medication to be injected through a port in the IV tubing just below the saline bag. They couldn't give it IV push which would have been an injection directly into a vein and had a quicker effect because she was seizing. That would have made it too difficult.

After it was done, the seizure quickly subsided and the patient was still again. They checked her vital signs on the electronic monitor. They had elevated rapidly during the seizure and then went back down as it dissipated.

They checked her breathing and for any drooling. The drooling had stopped and she appeared to be taking in oxygen okay. Her blood saturation level was 96, a definite improvement from earlier.

The doctor and nurses stayed there for a few minutes as the little girl's condition stabilized. Dr. Gray assigned one nurse to stay with her while he went to talk to her parents. Ron was doing all he could to keep

Wanda from climbing the walls in her fear for their child. It was fortunate that despite what had just occurred, the IV solutions, especially the anti-venom, was still running in her. Fortunately, the IV port on Penny's arm stayed in place, thanks to the stabilizing dressing which had been expertly applied and kept the port in place.

As the doctor talked with Ron and Wanda, the nurse monitored the child and the vital signs. She would not be left alone at any time because of the crisis still ongoing within her. Her body was fighting the venom with the help of its antagonist. It was the ultimate battle for her life.

Although the nurse had seen spider bite victims many times before, she hadn't seen a case like this. A multiple bite victim in a child was rare. One that came to the brink of death at least two or three times while being treated was even rarer. Penny was a special case and she'd be damned if this one didn't pull through. She would do all she could to ensure this beautiful little girl survived. She started by praying, while keeping her eyes on the girl and monitor.

Wanda had to ask the doctor why she had the seizure.

"We're not sure," he said. "Sometimes some venoms can cause this. Sometimes antivenoms as well. If a person has epilepsy, the venom can almost certainly trigger one to occur. It might be in your daughter's case that this brief seizure could have been caused by the battle that's going on in her body-her brain-between the venom and antivenom. If this was a one time event, then that's likely the case. If she has another seizure while on this third bottle, then a reaction to it might have developed within her."

Wanda and her husband looked at him with great concern. "Well what if she does? What do you do then?"

"At this point, Mrs. Worthington, I would recommend taking this one thing at a time. Let's see if this was the only event. We're monitoring her continuously and we'll know soon enough. I think this was a one-time event. We just have to wait for another 30 minutes to be sure. Excuse me while I go and check on another patient."

After the doctor had left, they walked back to their daughter who appeared to be sleeping peacefully. The nurses assured them her vital signs were near normal again and it was all downhill from here.

27

December 13, Sydney, 702 Australian Broadcasting Company

"Good morning. Once again we start the day with bright sunshine and a schedule that might meet your fancy, this morning. So grab your coffee and get comfy as we start today's Australian Style. This morning we have Bert Holfstrom who'll talk to us about his adventures in the Northern Territory and what he did to survive the outback in that area which, as you may know, isn't the most hospitable area. And later in the show, we have Angie Minster, who'll give us some tips on cooking fry-able foods without frying anything."

Victoria Rolley was a real go-starter on her daily morning television show. One of the qualities that people liked about her was her ability to catch the viewer's attention almost immediately. It was a combination of her personality, TV charisma, and interviewing skills that seemed to draw people in.

"But first we have a special guest from the University of Sydney, Doctor Mary Welling, a noted entomologist and arachnologist who'll be able to enlighten us non-experts on what's going on with this influx of the Sydney funnel web spider. As you may have heard on earlier reports this morning, a little girl from Goulburn was bitten multiple times allegedly by this species of spider. So far we know she's still in critical condition but stable. I don't think it needs to be said that our thoughts and prayers are with her and her parents. So, Doctor Welling, what do you make of all this?" she suddenly asked as she turned to her left to face Mary. "Was this poor little girl a victim of this funnel web outbreak? I understand that quite a few people had been bitten by these things that suddenly seemed to appear out of nowhere."

"Well, Vickie, I have to tell you that this outbreak was certainly unusual. These things, these types of spiders are indigenous to this area and therefore should be expected to be run into now and then. People are generally aware that they're here and usually take precautions to prevent confrontations.

"But in this case, the spider happened to be in its normal habitat at the time of the incident, rather than in the homes as the others were. Granted, they can get into homes as well. With the little girl, it was just a terrible misfortune that she stuck her hand in a nest, from what I gathered, that was where it could have been normally. As with the other cases, they were a bit unusual.

"For instance, what happened in the Ingram home was highly unusual and is difficult to explain. It certainly wasn't normal funnel web behavior and my department is researching into that to find out why they seemed to predate on humans. But I have a theory about that."

"Excuse me, doctor, did you say they were *predating* humans? *Hunting* humans? That seems to be pretty unbelievable and might be difficult for some to swallow. We're not their food source, right?"

"True, we are not and never will be. That would be impossible as anyone knows. However, I believe, although I can't be sure, that they seemed to be going after whoever was in their area. Apparently, someone had disturbed their nest and they don't like that. Because these spiders are extremely aggressive, even normally, I'm not really surprised they did that. As a result, that exterminator had succumbed to the bites unfortunately."

"So what about Tabitha Ingram who was killed by one of them? I don't really know the details about why she was attacked but could she have disturbed a nest as well?"

Mary wasn't sure about the answer to that one. She could only give her best educated guess.

"Well, no one knows for sure. But it's very possible. However, if she got too close to a web or nest, even unknowingly, the spider could have still considered her a threat. It wouldn't have known otherwise. If that was the case, it likely attacked the moment it got within range of her."

"I see. That certainly makes sense. So far there doesn't seem to be any plausible explanation, except the huge numbers of them in the Ingram case. We haven't seen that many in such a confined space in any of the other cases. Can you think of any reason for that? Do they normally herd together like that, for lack of a better word?"

"I've never heard of that happening before. However, there can be a plausible explanation for that too. They were in a small confined space. There may already have been a lot of eggs that hatched in that area; or, if they were already spiderlings that found that space, they may have found it an ideal area for food and it being a moist, cooler area than outside in the hot sun."

"One more question, Doctor Welling. How can we, the general public, avoid confrontation with these spiders to ensure our safety in our own homes? What can we do to protect ourselves and keep them from coming in?"

Mary then came out with all the standard precautions that apply not only to the funnel web but to all venomous creatures, including scorpions and snakes. Although there was a great deal to tell, she had only a few more seconds before they'd have to cut her. Before she knew it, the interview was over, the station cut to a commercial, and Vickie Rolley thanked her for her fascinating and helpful information and advice. A few minutes later, Mary was on her way to the school to prepare for her early afternoon class. She only hoped she didn't say anything wrong. Once you say something on TV, it's forever entrenched in viewers' minds and you can't retract it.

#

December 13, Blacktown, New South Wales

It was a long day for Rodney. Although he was able to focus on his work, at times he couldn't help thinking about what was going on at his house. It was mostly on his two allowed shift breaks and lunch period that his mind would wander to what was happening at home. His morning had gone fairly quickly because he had a lot of work to accomplish or at least get a good head start on, so that kept his mind off the time.

As he ate his sandwich, he thought that he probably wouldn't hear from them until the end of the day. If they had to go into that crawlspace, which would likely take a little time, he hoped they'd find the source of the spider problems and solve them once and for all. He didn't envy them at all for having to do that. According to what they told him, their suits were supposed to protect them from long, nail-like fangs. He hoped they were right. In the meantime, all he could do was continue to bide his time here, do his work and at the end of the day, go to the house to check on their progress.

On the radio that was playing nearby, he heard a report that caught his sudden attention.

"Here in Sydney, a little girl that was severely bitten by what was dubbed, the "death spider" yesterday afternoon in the back yard of her home remains in critical condition at Sydney Memorial Hospital. For reasons of privacy, the family requested her name not be publicized when questioned by reporters. So we'll call her Jane Doe.

"According to reports, she'd been bitten by the Sydney Funnel web spider when she stuck her hand apparently in a nest looking for a small ball that may have fallen into the hole. Paramedics were..."

Rodney heard enough. After gulping down the last of his sandwich, he got up from the table and walked outside. Holy Tamoley. That's the third of four incidents he heard about involving those things. At least the girl was still alive. Man, that's horrible, he thought to himself. Before his lunch half hour was over and he had to go back inside, he decided to call them at the cell number they gave him to find out their progress.

There was no answer, and the voice mail eventually picked up. Damn!

"John, this is Rod. Just calling to find out your progress. Wondering how the job is going. Give me a call soon as you get a chance. If I somehow miss your call, I'll be going to the house right from work. Give me a ring if you can in the meantime."

After hanging up, he figured well they might be real busy right now and can't answer the phone. Either that or they didn't hear it ring. Whatever, he told himself. A few minutes later, the signal for lunchtime over sounded from the loudspeaker and after discarding his lunch bag, he went back to work.

28

December 13, Central Coast, New South Wales

The hot dry day outside made Bradley Farrell keep his air conditioning going on inside. It was late morning, almost lunch time for him. It was the first of his two days off and he liked to spend it doing things that needed to be done while he had the time. Later he could relax.

He'd been with the force for nearly five years and he wouldn't trade his job for any other. Despite its dangers, he knew it was his calling. As a corporal for the Sydney Police Department, he was eligible to take the Sergeant's exam because he had the time in and certainly the experience. The exam wasn't coming up for another month or so and he had already put in for it.

After breakfast, he had started to work outside for a bit, tending to overgrown weeds around the one story two bedroom structure. His wife was off in Western Australia visiting family for a week so he had the place to himself. He'd known she had been looking forward to that for a while and was happy for her. Still, he missed the hell out of her and was looking forward to her return. They had no children because some years ago, not too long after they were married, she had to have a hysterectomy for a cyst on one of her ovaries and malformed Fallopian tubes which were too distorted to repair. They both accepted that and decided that if they wanted children in the future, they could always adopt one or two.

So far they hadn't. But they were still young. He was thirty-one and she was in her late twenties and there was no rush for now. Should they eventually make that decision, they wanted to be fully ready and prepared to take on the responsibility of parenthood.

Brad was sweating as he bent down to pull out more weeds from around the building. He stepped from one side of the front of the house to the other side, crossing the concrete platform that led into the house. Walking past the partially open screen door which tended to frequently stick open, he started his work on the other side. A half hour later, the weeds were out. After raking up the pulled plants, he loaded them into the wheelbarrow and dumped them into the edge of the area of trees at the far end of his backyard.

After spending another hour picking up small broken branches and other types of things one did to clear up one's lawn, he went back in the house to get a cold one. His feet were a little achy and sweaty, so he took his boots off and left them at the door. After retrieving the bottle of beer from the refrigerator, he decided to cool off for a bit, drink his beer, have lunch, and then use part of this afternoon to study for the Sergeant's exam.

Turning on the TV in the far right corner of his living room, he watched some of the programming which he normally didn't watch. It was almost time for the 12 noon news. As he looked at the screen, he thought he detected some movement in his left peripheral vision. It was just one of those things that makes you think you might have noticed something but then you might not have. He turned his head to look anyway, staring at the doorway and seeing the partially open screen door. He got up and manually closed it all the way. *One of these days I'm going to fix this thing.* He decided tomorrow would be a good day to do that. The door partially opened again. He hadn't closed it firmly enough against the door frame. It was another indication of a door in need of a minor but necessary repair.

After he went back to sit down on the sofa, the phone rang next to him.

"Hello?"

More movements in the doorway area which completely escaped his view.

"Hey, there, brother, how's your day off going so far?"

It was Tommy from the department. Coincidentally he had the day off too, although it was his second of the two.

Bradley filled him in all the light details. "And yours?" he asked.

"Listen, can I borrow you for just a very short time? Margie wants the bureau in our bedroom moved to the other end and that means pushing the bed to make room for it. Do you have time to give me a hand? If you don't, that's ok, I can call Charlie. You happen to be closer, that's why I called you first."

"Yea, that's fine. I can be there in about a half hour or so. That ok?"

"Hey, buddy, that's fine. Appreciate it. I'll have a cold beer for ya. Better yet, I'll make you lunch for your trouble. That is, I'll have Margie make us lunch."

"What's this about my making lunch?" Bradley could hear her voice in the background, almost echoing over the phone.

Bradley could hear the both of them talking and Margie readily agreed. "Ok, pal, come on over when you're ready. She will make us a fine lunch, guaranteed. And we're both grateful for your help. See ya in a bit, there matey."

"Righto. Be there shortly."

Now that a small part of his plans had changed, he took one more sip of his beer and decided to finish the rest later when he didn't have to go driving. Although Tommy lived only about ten minutes away, driving was still involved and he didn't want to feel tipsy in any way. He'd had only a few sips because he was a slow drinker so he knew he would be far from intoxicated.

He put the open bottle in the refrigerator, removed his sweaty shirt and put on a dry one, washed his face and combed his short, straight hair until he looked presentable enough to show up at somebody's house for lunch. Now to put his shoes back on and he would be ready to roll.

#

December 13, Sydney Memorial Hospital, New South Wales
The third anti-venom bottle was nearly finished. The nurse noticed movements in the young girl's eyes. Then her fingertips showed slight movements. She kept staring at her, hoping and wanting them to be movements of improvement rather than another possible seizure. They were subtle but there.

She called for the charge nurse and the doctor over the intercom. Within a minute they were both in there looking down at their patient and noticed the movements in the fingers increase until the hands started moving slowly. Then her eyes flickered, open and shut a few times, then opened and stayed open. They started focusing on whoever was looking down at her.

"Call the parents," barked the doctor. "Get them in here now!"

While the nurse ran to get them in the waiting room where they had been dozing waiting for word, the doctor spoke to Penny.

"Hi sweetheart. Can you hear me? Can you understand me?" Penny was looking at him, focusing her eyes on him. That was a very good sign, he realized. "I'm Doctor Billy." William Gray decided to make his communication with her as pleasant as he could considering the terrible trauma she'd just gone through. "I'm your doctor here and one of the people taking care of you. Can you talk to me? Just say yes."

As she stared back at him, her mouth moved, then sound came out. "Yes."

"Good. Good. How's your pain? Is it better, worse, or the same?" he asked her.

Then Penny's parents came running in. "Oh my baby, my baby, she's back with us," Wanda said, with tears of joy literally gushing out of her. Ron was smiling up a storm even with teary eyes also. "Oh, thank God."

It was a meeting that had been hoped for and prayed for the entire time she'd been there.

Gradually, the girl improved more. An hour later, the fourth and last bottle of anti-venom was hung and was soon infusing into her. By that time, Penny was more lucid and aware of what was going on. It was a very gradual but noticeable progression of improvement in a fairly quick amount of time once she first opened her eyes. Soon she was talking more and even smiling. The pain had subsided significantly. Although there was still some swelling in the hand area, it had gone down in size to the point where her hand almost looked normal again.

The antivenin had worked and none too soon. If there had been any kind of delay, even by just a few minutes, it could have been a very different outcome easily. As it turned out, their prayers were apparently answered and the girl pulled through by the skin of her teeth. It would not be long before the media got a hold of this news.

As for the Worthington family, they got their little girl back. In another day or two, she'd be discharged and on her way home, where her father had decided to set up fencing around what he considered "dangerous" areas so she wouldn't go wandering and this wouldn't happen again. It wouldn't be until the next day that Mary Welling would find out the good news that she, too, had hoped for.

29

December 13, Blacktown, New South Wales

After the end of the shift the whistle blew and Rod was soon out in his car. He tried calling the exterminators again but there still was no answer. Something was wrong, he could feel it. He left another message on John's voicemail and decided he better get there as soon as he could. The hell with the speed limits. It wasn't so much the house he was worried about: the fact was they were doing a very dangerous job. Had they both got hurt, bitten even? Did the crawlspace collapse on them? All kinds of things were running through his mind as he raced toward home to find out the truth.

"Son of a bitch," he muttered to himself out loud as he sped away from the plant and down the rural roads toward the city where he lived. He didn't know what he'd find except to see the house still standing there. But did his home now hide a deadly secret that was soon to be revealed? It normally took him about a half hour to get home. Today it was more like twenty minutes.

Normally, under other circumstances, he might not have been as concerned. But because of what they were dealing with, there was plenty of reason to be concerned. Especially after all he'd heard on the news. The landscape became a blur as he continued to bring that pedal closer to the metal. Fortunately for him, the roads were smooth and pretty straight. There appeared no other vehicles in the distance. It wouldn't be long now.

Central Coast, New South Wales

Good. One shoe on. Now the other. He put his foot into his right shoe. Initially he felt an object on the sole, then something like two needles piercing it. Then he felt the sensation of two hypodermic needles stabbing him followed quickly by the most excruciating pain he ever felt in his life.

"Ahhh!!!" He pulled his foot out and turned his shoe upside down. Out fell the largest spider he'd ever seen. It was crushed flat from his foot bearing down on it, but he knew instantly that he'd been stung.

As a sometimes first responder himself, he knew right away what to do. Picking up the phone, he called for emergency medical services to send an ambulance and the reason. Then he called Tommy and told him what happened.

"Oh my God! Hey man, I'll be right there. Don't move or walk around. Stay put and off that foot until the ambulance gets there. I'll see if I can get there sooner to help you. I'm going to hang up so I can get going. Marge!" Then the phone clicked to a dial tone.

The pain was terrible. Having learned first aid, and about the deadly creatures that sometimes confronted people with their nasty stings or bites, he knew enough to know that it was no scorpion. He wasn't sure if it was a wolf spider, a black house spider, or something worse. He couldn't tell for sure because it had been flattened by his weight. But he knew the hospital would want the specimen so he kept it right where he left it, rather than try to jar it. For now, he had to limit his movements which would have the same effect as the venom now in his body.

As he waited the terrible long minutes for help to arrive, the pain increased and he started feeling numbness and tingling around his mouth. As he sat on the sofa as still as he could, soon muscle twitching started which he could not control. His vision started becoming blurry and doubled. As his eyes rolled back and forth, he tried to regain focus and awareness of what he was seeing. In the light coming from the doorway area, he saw, or thought he saw a number of large black things crawling slowly toward him. With his vision blurred and doubled, he didn't know what he was seeing, but even so they were scary-looking enough to him for him to shout out in panic. It was like he was living his worst nightmare. With the pain progressively increasing, and his twitching becoming worse, was he hallucinating as well? The things looked bigger now and closer to him. He cringed up on the crouch terrified of what was going on with him and whether or not those things would get to him. If they did, what would happen?

As he looked at the things closer to the sofa now, they looked huge and more numerous. His eyes were now watering as well. He started breathing harder. His eyes were now like wide open saucers as he realized he was in very serious trouble. If someone didn't get here soon, he was thinking he could die. The pain now spread from his feet to his arms and started entering his torso. It was a combination of searing hot and stabbing sharp pain that didn't subside but got only worse.

There was nothing he could do. Despite the tortuous agony he was enduring, his mind was still clear. He was at the mercy of circumstances and whether or not help could arrive in time to save his life. He didn't know whether he was suffering from an anaphylaxis reaction or whether it was a bite that was deadly to everyone. He was not a spider or bug expert. Whatever it was that bit him was certainly not something that was compatible with humans or other animals.

He started to become slightly groggy. He heard a loud bang at the doorway. His watery eyes tried to focus, but all he could make out was a tall dark figure in the doorway. "Holy shit! What the hell? Holy mother of…Hey buddy, stay right there. I'll get something right outside your doorway. Won't hurt ya but will get them away from ya. Stay right there matey."

Tommy ran to the hose connected to the faucet outside. He turned the handle on the faucet itself to get the water running. Although he had forgotten in his haste to check the hose handle, he didn't care. His pal was in trouble and he had to do something now. As he pulled it to and through the front door, the ambulance pulled in. He yelled to the medics to standby, there were killer spiders in there threatening to do his friend in. They came into the front yard with the stretcher and bags of equipment but stood by in surprised awe and concern. They no doubt were wondering why the water hose.

Tommy sprayed the water onto the living room floor. "Jeez, I'm sorry buddy. With all those sons of bitches down there, this is the only thing I could do."

The water flooded the living room floor, washing away the small army of arachnids that had invaded and threatened Bradley. He never realized he was doing exactly the right thing to kill them or at least get them out of there. After the area to the sofa was cleared, at least temporarily, he called the paramedics in.

"Careful. I had to flood the place. The floor was full of bloody big spiders. Nasty little sons of bitches. Looks like my friend here is in trouble. Please take care of him."

They ran to him, quickly checked him out. His BP and heart rate were alarmingly elevated. When they also quickly saw visual signs of his medical crisis, they had time to figure out what was wrong. Putting him on the stretcher, they whisked him to the ambulance as quickly as they could, and put him in, strapped down safely for the twenty-minute ride to Sydney Memorial, which was the closest hospital. Tommy watched helplessly. Just before they drove off, the medic in the passenger side told him that he might have just saved his life. A minute later they were off, already notifying the emergency room of the case and ETA. Tommy called his wife and explained what was going on. The bureau would have to wait. He was going to the hospital to find out more about what was happening with his friend.

At the time, in the chaos and haste of trying to save Brad's life, no one realized that something important had been missed that was crucial for Bradley's treatment. The hospital would be the first to know and Tommy would be the second.

#

Sydney, New South Wales

On arrival at his house, he saw the Gone for Good vehicle still there. The house had the same benign peaceful look as it always did. As Rod knew, however, and as most people did, looks could be deceiving. Before he got out of his car, he decided to call them again mainly to see if they would answer the phone this time. After three rings, the phone was answered but mechanically only. No voice said hello or anything else on the other end.

"Hello? Hello, John. Is that you?" Only dead silence met his ears. There wasn't even any background noise of any kind. *What the hell is going on here?* "Hello?" he tried again but with the same results. He hung up. Maybe his signal was getting through but theirs weren't. That was certainly possible. He called one more time. The phone answered again but again there was no voice response. It reminded him of an episode of the old TV show, the Twilight Zone.

Getting out of his car quickly, he walked toward the front of the house. He decided not to go inside. At least not yet. Strolling past the exterminator vehicle, he saw they were not inside it. Continuing on toward the backyard, he stopped when he saw the dug up spot where he figured it led down to the crawlspace. On the top edge of the dirt he saw a number of black things. Initially he didn't know what they were and possibly thought they might be rocks or something. But he saw one of those "rocks" move and it had legs. Many legs. *Oh shit.*

".John, John are you guys down there?"

Suddenly a voice burst through the silence from down below. "Yes. Yea, Mr. Johnson we're down here. Sorry we couldn't talk on the phone."

"Call me Rod. Are you guys ok?"

"So far so good. We're kinda in a pickle, as you can see."

Rod stared at the black things, now knowing what they really were. Why were they there like that? He was no expert but that was certainly not normal by any stretch of the imagination.

"What happened? Why couldn't you talk on the phone?" he asked.

John then went on to explain that when they had gotten down there, they found a huge funnel web that was the biggest web they'd ever seen. It was nearly as big as a man and almost as wide. They immediately destroyed it with water. They saw only a couple of the Sydney Funnel web spiders so they used water to first disorientate them and then drown them. They hadn't, couldn't have known, that there were many more of them housed there and they were not home at the moment when the two men went down there.

Rod looked at the line of spiders along the top edge of the dirt pile. They were no doubt an immediate threat to the two men down in the space. At any moment they could crawl down there. Perhaps the suits would protect them as they had mentioned to him. So if that was the case, then they shouldn't have a problem. So why were they so afraid to put the phone to their mouth and talk? It didn't make sense. For the time being, he kept his distance.

"John, I thought you said you were wearing suits that couldn't be penetrated by their teeth; excuse me, their fangs."

"Yea, tell me about it. Those suits are identical in appearance as regular suits. The only difference is on the label inside the top part. For the anti-penetrating suit, it has the letters APS imprinted on it which doesn't fade or wash away. It's permanent. The regular suits don't have that. Other than that, they look exactly the same."

"So don't tell me: you grabbed the wrong ones," Rod said, already figuring that's what happened.

"You guessed it. And now we're paying the price for that little guffaw of ours."

"Ok. Before we go any further on this, let me see what I can do to get those buggers away from you. I'm obviously not going to wash them with water. The water would just push them down onto you. From the little I learned, they're not jumpers so I don't think they'll jump or parachute down to you." That word caused a slight smirk on John's face. "Good one, Rod. Let me think."

Rod already thought of something and it didn't take a rocket scientist or arachnologist to figure this one out. Going to his shed in the backyard, he went to get the tool he needed to do the job.

30

December 13, Sydney Memorial Hospital ER, New South Wales

After speaking with one of the ER nurses there, Tommy learned that they were doing all they could to take care of Mr. Farrell she told him.

"He was bitten, ma'am. It looked like one of those things that they reported on the TV news."

"Yes, we think so too," she said. "But we need proof that the Sydney funnel web was responsible."

"Proof? Why? And what proof do you need?"

"Did you see it bite him?"

"Course not. I wasn't there."

"Can you get us a specimen of it if you can find a dead one?"

Tommy thought for a moment. He had washed them away from Bradley so the medics could get to the sofa. Then he also remembered Brad telling him that he had gotten bitten when he put his foot in his shoe. Although he didn't say which shoe, if it was dead he'd find it there.

"I'll get it for you. How come you need that?"

"Before we give the anti-venom, we have to be 100% sure it's the correct one. If we give the wrong one from another species, it will likely kill him."

"I'm on my way. Be back soon as I can."

Before he walked out the door, he stopped suddenly and turned around.

"Nurse, can you tell me one thing?"

"Sure, if I can."

"What will they do if I *can't* find a specimen, not even a dead one?"

The nurse just looked at him with a sheepish grin. There was no indication if she knew the answer to that or not. "Better get going. Time is not on your friend's side. Just don't get into an accident." He suspected she did know, and ran out the door anyway.

Tommy didn't care about speed limits at this point. If he got stopped he'd explain to the cops what would happen if he didn't get the thing back there pretty quickly. Chances are, they'd escort him with lights and maybe sirens to the house.

As it turned out, he got there in record time without being stopped. The door was still unlocked and the front area was still wet. Even though he had to make this fast, he was able to keep his presence of mind and tread cautiously inside the wet living room. He looked for his friend's shoe. They were separated on the floor off to the right of the door. It was the left one. Looking inside, he saw it was empty. Further inside, he saw the right shoe against one of the walls.

Knowing what might be inside of it, whether dead or alive, gave him the creepiest feeling he'd ever had. Cautiously he bent his head over to see inside of it and saw a black object just to the right of the shoe on the floor. The legs were all crumpled up. This was it! That was the thing that nearly killed his friend.

He looked around quickly for a dustpan, brush, and bag to put the creature in. He wasn't about to pick that thing up with his hand. Damn, it was creepy looking even dead.!

Finding them, he gingerly picked up the dead spider and put it inside the plastic bag. He made sure the bag was secured tight. Despite it being dead, it still gave him the creeps and he had thoughts of it coming back to life, ripping through the bag with its huge fangs and stabbing him with them. He ended up tying the bag at the top no less than three times. Then he inserted it into another plastic bag, just for good measure he decided.

#

Rod found the shovel pretty quickly and got a wheelbarrow as well. Running back toward the pile, he found another area of ground to dig some dirt up. After putting a load of dirt into the wheelbarrow and filling it with a heaping pile he quickly calculated and decided it was a sufficient amount to do the job. He'd have to do it quickly and nonstop. Those things could move fast and were as aggressive as they were speedy. It would have been better if he had a helper, but he didn't. So he had to do the best that he possibly could.

Cautiously and slowly he moved the wheelbarrow until he got as close as he could safely get to the line of spiders that were still looking down at the two men. The sight was as incredible as it was terrifying. It was if they were trying to decide how to get down there. As to why the men couldn't talk on the phone, he'd have to find that out later.

Ready, set, go! Fast and furious he shoveled the dirt onto the spiders. Some of them were trying to scurry away on the other end. He saw that and hit them with the dirt one shovel after another. He didn't stop shoveling the dirt onto them until after he had emptied the wheelbarrow. Quickly looking for any escapees, he saw none and gave the signal for the men to quickly come up. Seeing the foot ladder on the side he lowered it down to them. They came up and thanked him for his quick thinking. But John had to get back to business despite the offset of their initial plans.

"Rod, we need to more fully hose that area down. Let me do that now. If there are any more lingering spiders down there, we need to get them now. It means your crawlspace will be flooded for a while. These critters don't like water or swimming very much so hopefully it'll keep them out. You might want to consider filling the crawlspace up so it's no more, or wall it with strong concrete with concrete stairs and a door with spaces around it that won't let these things in anymore. At least not the adults. Not much nowadays is spider proof or bug proof. But you can at least make it more difficult for them."

Rod agreed. He'd have to think about whether to fill it or concrete wall it. But he was grateful that they were gotten rid of. He knew more could return at some later date, if he allowed that to happen. There was no way he would. After what they did to Max and almost to Friskie, he decided he would have a house that was as close to being as spider proof and bug proof as it could get.

#

Sydney Memorial Hospital

An hour after Tommy had left to get the specimen, the first bottle of anti-venom pumped into Brad's body after the specimen was confirmed to be the Sydney Funnel Web spider. He was semiconscious, in pain, with the telltale symptoms of full envenomation. Along with the anti-venom drip was the hydration drip of normal saline. He'd also received intramuscular injections of narcotic pain medications and Ativan to prevent any seizures and control the onset of any anxiety at the same time.

Because he had received the proper treatment in a timely manner, his prognosis for a full recovery was good. Because his symptoms were severe but not as severe as they could have been, he was prescribed three bottles of the anti-venom, with a fourth on standby if it was determined he needed it.

Tommy was glad about the news. At the same time, he wondered how he could get a hold of Barbara. He knew she was off on the other side of the country visiting family there. But he didn't have the phone number or where she was staying. He'd have to wait until Brad was lucid and able to talk.

He'd also have a talk with him about a full extermination of his house and taking preventive measures against future invasions. And, in addition getting that damn front door fixed. All in due time, he thought.

This crisis would eventually be over and he wanted this all a part of the past and a learning experience.

Eventually he left the hospital building, leaving them with his phone number to contact him. It would be at least another twelve to sixteen hours before Brad would be lucid enough and aware enough to talk. Tomorrow he would check on him and it would be a better day. He just knew it. As soon as he got in the car and before he left the parking lot, he would contact the PD and let them know what happened to one of their own and where he presently was. The multitude of visits from brother officers would begin tomorrow.

31

December 14, University of Sydney, New South Wales

The group was that of seven; scientists from various areas of Australia who were all entomologists. Mary was one of the two arachnid specialists that were there. Eric Robertson was sitting at the edge of the long table and soon their discussion was underway. It turned out that Dean Minson was right. This would be more of a think tank to figure out the cause of the present situation and come up with some kind of preventive plan for the future. At this point, Mary wished she were back in the classroom or doing her studies in the lab rather than sitting at a table and coming up with ideas. This was really not her thing. But being the situation as it was, she would.

CONCLUSION

December 22, New South Wales

In the end, it was determined that the unusual breakout of Sydney Funnel Web spiders could not be blamed on any one specific factor, but several of them. For one thing, people had become complacent to their presence around the area and were lax more than usual in using preventive measures to keep their homes and yards safe from these predatory creatures. They'd been around for so long and so few had been bitten on the average over the past several years that they had been almost forgotten.

Mary Welling and her colleague Tom had considered the fact that those spiderling escapees more than likely contributed to the problem, at least around the area surrounding the university. Not likely further out. At the conference, she decided to relate the story about the spiderling escapees to the group.

This season was drier and hotter than normal with insufficient rainfall to keep them under cover in the areas where they normally inhabited. Seeking cooler areas that provided some measure of protection from the hot blistering Australian sun, it was likely they ended up intruding into people's homes and other areas that would increase their confrontations with people. Thus, this year was different than most other years in the past.

Although the spiders would always be out there and confrontations would still occur, with the media and other sources of important information about these spiders educating the public via broadcasting and printouts, reports of bites had decreased significantly. They didn't stop and never would. But things seemed to be going back to normal again overall.

As for Penny Worthington, the little girl pulled through. After four days in the hospital she was discharged from home. Constant prayers from her parents and all her friends and the rest of her family were certainly answered. She had come as close to death as any person could under the circumstances. Soon she was back playing with her friends. Her father had constructed small fence lines along the wood areas in the backyard. Penny and everyone else were strictly forbidden to go beyond that for any reason. If a ball went over the low fencing, she was to leave it there and let her father know. This rule applied to all her friends and everyone else as well.

John and his partner from Gone for Good Extermination Company continued their work as usual not letting something like that scary incident deter them from their chosen occupation.

Rod reoccupied his home again but with almost paranoiac cautiousness. He was forever leery of dark shadowy areas. Any cracks or crevices he discovered he'd immediately spray with some kind of bug spray that would kill any creepy crawlies until he could fix them as soon as possible. He made sure the cracks under his doors leading to the outside were blocked by some kind of cloth barricade. Chances are they were too narrow for any venomous spiders like the funnel web. Nevertheless he didn't want to take any chances. As for his crawlspace, he had it filled in completely. That was one less area he'd have to worry about and would make it impossible for the same incident to reoccur.

Despite his fears from what had occurred, he felt he and Friskie would now be considerably safer than they had been. With Friskie having become "acquainted" with their previous unwanted intruders, he believed she would now be a good first alert system should any more intrude into their home.

Peter and Sandy were now back in their home. A couple months later he put his home up for sale. His fear of going downstairs never left him and he decided he didn't want to have to live with that there in addition to the memory of his wife having died in that area. Eventually he hoped to find a house in another area of town so that Sandy didn't have to change schools. Until they moved, he would use the nearest Laundromat to do their laundry. Although they were still grieving and would for a while, knowing they had each other kept them going. Peter made sure he did his best to keep Sandy's spirits up. For a child to endure the tragic loss of her mother was heartbreaking. His contact with school counselors and therapists, as well as having her visit them for sessions would hopefully help her cope with the sadness and grief she was undergoing.

Bradley Farrell pulled through after completing his treatment of three bottles of anti-venom. They kept him an extra day just to make sure he really was ok and no side effects would occur from the infusions. He had received multiple visits from his police colleagues, including the police chief. He believed the entire department had gone to the hospital to see him. Never had he felt so grateful for the men and women he worked with. To him it was surely a blessing. And the same for having a friend like Tommy who he believed had saved his life.

The day before he was to be discharged, he called Barbara to let her know what had happened. As expected she was shocked and deeply disturbed, especially since she hadn't been there for him. He assured her that he was fine now and it was his own stupid laxness that contributed to his injury and hospitalization. After explaining everything else related to the incident he told her he was going to fix everything that needed fixing, especially whatever led to the outdoors. He promised her he'd do everything he could to ensure that they would no longer have any unwanted visitors. As a last word, he re-emphasized that she didn't need to return home until her planned date. He'd be perfectly fine and had Tommy to confer with if needed. That seemed to satisfy her.

Overall, the panic in the area that had been on the increase appeared to stop in its progress and began to subside almost ten days after the first incident. People started to relax again. Things were returning back to the way they were.

#

In the small patch of woods bordering the outback outside of Sydney, the large underground den was full of life. After mating the male spiders left for good to hunt, bite, and kill whatever they needed. Even with the males gone, the numerous females remained in the cool darkness. After the appropriate time had passed they laid their eggs. In time, these would hatch and hundreds of spiderlings would emerge to help populate the den. Once they were matured and experienced the necessary moltings with their growth, they too would eventually leave the nest to hunt, bite, and kill. They would have no idea what humans were or that they even existed. Many of them would almost certainly find out. Because of the time of a spider's life, that would be sooner than they realized. And the world around them would be reminded once again that they were here to stay.

After about six months from returning to the house, Peter Ingram sold it. He and Sandy moved to a condo which he bought on the other side of town. Since the incident, a large percentage of the public has become more vigilant for the creatures. That and taking preventive measures is all they can do. After the dust settled, life returned to normal for most people.

CHECK OUT OTHER GREAT HORROR NOVELS

BLACK FRIDAY
by Michael Hodges

Jared the kleptomaniac, Chike the unemployed IT guy, Patricia the shopaholic, and Jeff the meth dealer are trapped inside a Chicago supermall on Black Friday. Bridgefield Mall empties during a fire alarm, and most of the shoppers drive off into a strange mist surrounding the mall parking lot. They never return. Chike and his group try calling friends and family, but their smart phones won't work, not even Twitter. As the mist creeps closer, the mall lights flicker and surge. Bulbs shatter and spray glass into the air. Unsettling noises are heard from within the mist, as the meth dealer becomes unhinged and hunts the group within the mall. Cornered by the mist, and hunted from within, Chike and the survivors must fight for their lives while solving the mystery of what happened to Bridgefield Mall. Sometimes, a good sale just isn't worth it.

GRIMWEAVE
by Tim Curran

In the deepest, darkest jungles of Indochina, an ancient evil is waiting in a forgotten, primeval valley. It is patient, monstrous, and bloodthirsty. Perfectly adapted to its hot, steaming environment, it strikes silent and stealthy, it chosen prey: human. Now Michael Spiers, a Marine sniper, the only survivor of a previous encounter with the beast, is going after it again. Against his better judgement, he is made part of a Marine Force Recon team that will hunt it down and destroy it.

The hunters are about to become the hunted.

CHECK OUT OTHER GREAT HORROR NOVELS

DEATH CRAWLERS
by Gerry Griffiths

Worldwide, there are thought to be 8,000 species of centipede, of which, only 3,000 have been scientifically recorded. The venom of Scolopendra gigantea—the largest of the arthropod genus found in the Amazon rainforest—is so potent that it is fatal to small animals and toxic to humans. But when a cargo plane departs the Amazon region and crashes inside a national park in the United States, much larger and deadlier creatures escape the wreckage to roam wild, reproducing at an astounding rate. Entomologist, Frank Travis solicits small town sheriff Wanda Rafferty's help and together they investigate the crash site. But as a rash of gruesome deaths befalls the townsfolk of Prospect, Frank and Wanda will soon discover how vicious and cunning these new breed of predators can be. Meanwhile, Jake and Nora Carver, and another backpacking couple, are venturing up into the mountainous terrain of the park. If only they knew their fun-filled weekend is about to become a living nightmare.

THE PULLER
by Michael Hodges

Matt Kearns has two choices: fight or hide. The creature in the orchard took the rest. Three days ago, he arrived at his favorite place in the world, a remote shack in Michigan's Upper Peninsula. The plan was to mourn his father's death and figure out his life. Now he's fighting for it. An invisible creature has him trapped. Every time Matt tries to flee, he's dragged backwards by an unseen force. Alone and with no hope of rescue, Matt must escape the Puller's reach. But how do you free yourself from something you cannot see?

CHECK OUT OTHER GREAT HORROR NOVELS

MONSTROSITY
by Tim Curran

The Food. It seeped from the ground, a living, gushing, teratogenic nightmare. It contaminated anything that ate it, causing nature to run wild with horrible mutations, creating massive monstrosities that roam the land destroying towns and cities, feeding on livestock and human beings and one another. Now Frank Bowman, an ordinary farmer with no military skills, must get his children to safety. And that will mean a trip through the contaminated zone of monsters, madmen, and The Food itself. Only a fool would attempt it. Or a man with a mission.

THE SQUIRMING
by Jack Hamlyn

You are their hosts

You are their food.

The parasites came out of nowhere, squirming horrors that enslaved the human race. They turned the population into mindless pack animals, psychotic cannibalistic hordes whose only purpose was to feed them.

Now with the human race teetering at the edge of extinction, extermination teams are fighting back, killing off the parasites and their voracious hosts. Taking them out one by one in violent, bloody encounters.

The future of mankind is at stake.

And time is running out.